A RAT'S TALE

TOR SEIDLER

Pictures by
FRED MARCELLINO

HARPERTROPHY
A DIVISION OF HARPERCOLLINS PUBLISHERS

This work was originally published in 1986
by Farrar, Straus & Giroux
Published by arrangement with Farrar, Straus & Giroux, Inc.

A Rat's Tale
Text copyright © 1986 by Tor Seidler
Pictures copyright © 1986 by Fred Marcellino
All rights reserved
Library of Congress catalog card number: 98-31781
Printed in the United States of America
First Harper Trophy edition, 1999

A RAT'S TALE

On a sticky midsummer day, when the heat and humidity kept most of the creatures in Central Park from stirring, a young rat named Montague Mad-Rat—or, to be precise, Montague Mad-Rat the Younger—was busy collecting feathers in the birds' preening grounds above the reservoir. Once his tail was looped around as many feathers as it could manage, Montague crept through the underbrush down to the berry patches by the Great Lawn. Here he carefully gathered up ripe, fallen berries into his mouth, choosing the widest possible selection of colors. These were for his mother, who melted the berries down into dyes to color the feathers, which she fashioned into rather fanciful shapes best described, perhaps, as rat hats.

When his cheeks were bulging, Montague headed for home. The quickest way was by an underground drainpipe that came up in Columbus Circle, at the foot of the great park. But it always took him quite a while to get there because of his zigzagging route under bushes and park benches. Montague dreaded like the plague meeting other young rats. If they ever caught sight of him, they poked fun at him. Not that he really blamed them, considering his puffy cheeks and the bouquet of feathers in his tail. But once, about a year ago, he'd introduced himself to a group of young wharf rats in the park *before* he'd collected any feathers or berries, and they'd pointed and laughed at him anyway. Something was obviously the matter with him—but what? This mystery, haunting him ever since, had turned him painfully shy.

On this particular summery afternoon, Montague had made his winding way only halfway down the park when the air grew very still. It was almost as if the sky were holding its breath. He poked his snout out from under a forsythia bush and looked across the Sheep Meadow. It was sheepless, as usual, sprinkled with the regular huge human children holding ice-cream cones and balloons. But a faint sound came from the distance, as of a rat scampering over a tin roof. Suddenly there was a clap of thunder. The sky seemed to take this as a signal to stop holding its breath. The faint scampering sound grew into a loud rustling, and all the trees around the meadow bowed their heads before a driving wind. As the human children ran for cover, they let go of their colorful balloons. The balloons went up, the raindrops came down. They met, and the rain won, bursting all the balloons in a second.

By the time Montague finally came out of the park onto Columbus Circle, his sleek gray fur was soaked, and he'd lost half his mother's feathers. Columbus Circle was in a turmoil. Yellow cabs and delivery trucks were honking, and drenched people were rushing every which way, making it a decidedly unpleasant spot to linger. But just as Montague was about to dive off the curb into the shelter of an underground drainpipe, something caught his sharp eyes. A prim pack of rats was stranded under the towering statue in the center of the Circle, huddled under brightly colored umbrellas. Montague was surprised: he'd never seen rats with umbrellas before. A giant bus rolled up to the statue. One after the next, the rats leapt up onto the bus's back bumper, where they sat in a neat row, still holding their umbrellas over their heads. As the bus pulled away, a strong gust of wind caught the umbrella of the rat seated on the far end of the bumper. This umbrella went sailing and tumbling through the air, high over the traffic.

It landed below the curbstone a yard from where Montague crouched. Clinging to the handle was a young she-rat with bewitchingly beady eyes, which she blinked, as if mildly startled. She gave a sneeze as she climbed onto the curb, and then with her free forepaw she evened the bow of a blue ribbon that was tied around her neck. Montague had never seen a rat wearing a ribbon before.

"Gad, that was different," she said, smiling at him from under the rim of her umbrella, which was made of shiny plastic. "Did you see me?"

Thanks to the berries clogging his mouth, all Montague could do was nod.

"It was pretty exciting," she confessed. "Are you a wharf rat, too?"

He nodded again.

"I thought so, but you look so awfully dark, and your cheeks . . . No offense, but they're like a chipmunk's. Did you leave your umbrella home?"

Since he had no umbrella to his name, it was a hard question to answer without resorting to words. He simply smiled. She broke into a bright laugh.

"You'll have to excuse me," she said, her gray eyes twinkling beadily. "But your smile . . . Where *did* you get those cheeks?"

He stopped smiling.

"Oh, I didn't mean to offend you! It's just the cheeks, and the feathers, and no umbrella, when all those clouds were piling up across the river this morning."

The thought of it all made her giggle uncontrollably. She clapped a paw over her snout to stop herself. Just then, another strong gust of wind swept across Columbus Circle, and it jerked the umbrella out of her other paw. The umbrella sailed away into the park,

over the bowing treetops, growing smaller and smaller until it disappeared in the rainy distance like a bird migrating north for the summer.

"I'll be!" she said.

Now that the young she-rat's fur was in danger of getting as soaked as his, Montague extended a paw toward the grating, inviting her to slip through ahead of him. She stared at him curiously.

"You want me to cross the street?" she asked, blinking raindrops out of her eyes. "Hadn't I better wait for the light?"

Montague motioned more dramatically downward.

"Oh, dear," she said. "Did you lose a penny down there? Gad, what a field trip! I'm getting drenched to the bone!"

The time had come, Montague felt, to throw good manners to the wind. Motioning her to follow, he leapt onto the grating and slipped through, landing on the bank of a rushing underground stream in the drainage pipe. There he waited, staring back up. Eventually, a slightly turned-up snout and a pair of beady eyes appeared in a slit in the grate.

"Are you down there?" she called. "I can't see a single thing!"

"I'm right here!" he replied. And, really, it was a relief that she couldn't see, for when he spoke his jaws crushed some of the berries and berry juice began to dribble down his snout.

"Are you still in one piece?" she inquired. "I'm sorry you slipped."

"But I didn't slip. Whereabouts do you live, miss?"

"Number 11, Wharf 62."

"Well, hop on down. I'll walk you home."

"Down in a *gutter*?"

Montague stared around at the underground cavern. "You don't want to walk up in the rain, do you?" he asked.

"Your voice!" she said, giggling.

Indeed, the berries did make his voice slurpy. Why, oh why, did he have to have them in his mouth right now? Still, he repeated his offer. "But I should introduce myself first," he added. "I'm Montague Mad-Rat."

"You're not really."

"Yes, I am."

"But what a funny name! No offense."

"May I ask yours?"

Again, the bright, good-natured laugh tinkled down from above. Never had Montague run across a rat who found things so amusing.

"You'd still be a stranger," she reasoned, "and I'm afraid Mother doesn't let me go places with strangers, especially not gutters."

A traffic light changed up on Columbus Circle. Taxis and trucks came rumbling around. Squishing through a newly formed puddle, they sent great muddy arches of water into the air, one of which landed squarely on the grate.

In the dimness of the gutter, all Montague saw was a blur of paws—but he heard the splash. The lovely rat had fallen into the rushing underground current! As it was about to sweep her away, he threw her his tail, sacrificing the rest of his mother's feathers, which were carried off downstream in an instant.

"Gad!" cried the drenched young rat as she pulled herself onto the bank. "That *was* different!"

"Are you all right?" Montague asked.

She let his tail drop. "All right? I'm fine—except that my fur's soaked, umbrella gone, ribbon shot, bus missed, and I'm dripping in a gutter on the verge of pneumonia!"

"I'm terribly sorry."

"Sorry? But you didn't do anything."

"Oh, thank you."

"What for?"

"For . . . for not blaming me."

She clapped her muddy paws together. "Is it a family trait, or what? Your voice, I mean."

"Oh, no, it's only . . . you see . . . my mouth is full of berries."

"Berries! But how loathsome! I've never heard of a wharf rat eating berries. Are you sure you're a wharf rat?"

"I'm positive."

"You do have a nice long tail."

"Thank you."

"Do you suppose this water has germs?"

"It's only rainwater."

"Oh. Mother says you never know where you might pick up germs. Have you been down in this ghastly place before?"

"I come down here almost every day. It's the quickest way home."

"I'll be! Where do you live?"

"Well . . . not so far from Wharf 62, really."

The grating overhead shuddered, and so did she.

"What was that?"

"Just the traffic."

"It gives me the creeps. Will you please take me home now?"

Montague assured her that it would be an honor, and he led the way along the bank of the underground stream. Two or three times every block, he glanced back over his shoulder to see the lovely pair of beady eyes shining just behind him in the dimness. Her voice was wonderful company, too, as she chattered about her field trip and answered his question about her umbrella, explaining that it came from a bar-supply store.

"Did you sneak into the store yourself?" he asked, amazed.

"Me? Are you serious?"

"Oh. Your father?"

"What? Daddy doesn't have time for snooping around like that. He picks them up from pack rats."

"Oh."

Before long, Montague led the way up through another grate. The waterfront was directly across the street. The rain had stopped, the sky had cleared, and the pavement gave off a pleasant, scrubbed smell.

"That *was* quick!" she exclaimed, standing beside him on the curb.

Montague pointed across the street. "There's Wharf 62."

"Well, I can *see* that. Do you have a snoutbleed?"

Lowering his snout, Montague wiped a paw across the drool. "No, that's only berry juice," he mumbled, shamefaced.

"You and your berries! But what's become of your feathers?"

"Oh, I didn't really want them."

She was keeping an eye on the traffic. As it cleared, she started to creep down from the curb, then suddenly stopped. "But you dropped them for my sake, didn't you? When you pulled me out of the muck?"

Montague shrugged. She crept up and gave him a kiss on the snout. Then she turned and scurried gracefully across the street into one of those grand wharves that stretch so far out onto the river.

While Montague was collecting his mother's supplies, most other young rats in New York City were out scouring the streets for pennies. But Montague knew very few other young rats. When he wasn't creeping around the park, he was at home. Of course, he'd struck up a few stray conversations in gutters. But until this afternoon he'd never seen—not to mention talked to—a young rat as lovely and extraordinary as . . . but, of course, she hadn't even told him her name.

As if drawn by her charm, Montague followed

where she'd gone, across the street, into a slit between the padlocked, sliding doors of the wharf.

Inside the slit, a suspicious voice addressed him. "Yeeees? And whom might you be looking for?"

Montague peered left and right but saw no one. "I'm looking for number 11," he replied experimentally.

"Eleven, eh."

Only when Montague dropped his glance did he find the dormouse. The dormouse was standing up straight as a soldier, but even perfect posture couldn't make up for his tiny size.

"Are the Moberly-Rats expecting you?" the dormouse inquired.

"No," Montague said, thrilled at the mere sound of her last name. "But if—"

"Good heavens, rat!" the dormouse shrieked. "You're bleeding on my lobby!"

Montague wiped his snout again. He hadn't realized the dusty concrete expanse was a lobby. "I'm terribly sorry. It's only berry juice."

"Well, the least you could do is stand outside!"

Montague backed out of the lobby.

"These rats," the dormouse muttered as he occupied the slit. "Now, which of the Moberly-Rats did you want?"

"I'm not . . . quite sure."

"You're not quite sure. And who shall I say is calling? Are you quite sure who *you* are?"

At this point, Montague began to consider his condition. For some strange reason, there was nothing in the world he cared about just now except seeing the lovely young Moberly-Rat again—and yet he realized that in his current damp, drooly state it would only be a disaster if he tried. So, turning his tail, he crept sadly away, while at his back the erect little mouse complained some more about rats.

After slipping back through the grate across the street, Montague followed an underground stream for a few blocks and then turned down a cracked concrete pipe. As he pattered along, the air grew thick with smoke. Soon he was home.

Long ago, the earth had caved in on a weak spot in the concrete sewer, and it was at this dead end that the Mad-Rat family lived. Enthroned high on the slope of mud forming the back wall of their house was Mr. Mad-Rat, hard at work on a mud castle—his hundred and seventh. The other hundred and six castles were arrayed on the slope beneath him. Mrs. Mad-Rat, meanwhile, shuffled around down below, poking smoky fires smoldering under soup cans. As she went from can to can, she tripped over her younger children, and was quite deaf to the screams of her youngest—half a dozen blind, hairless ratlings curled up in a sardine tin at the foot of the slope of mud castles. Mrs. Mad-Rat's fur was covered with bits of plumage, and bright feather hats hung on the rounded, concrete walls of the pipe. Montague was perfectly ac-

customed to the screaming and the castles and the smoke and the feathered rat hats, but this afternoon, for some reason, he felt a bit hemmed in by it all.

"Thank goodness!" Mrs. Mad-Rat cried over the shrill ratlings as he emerged from the smoke.

"I'm sorry I'm so late, Mother. There was this storm, and—"

"Why are you talking, Monty?" said Mrs. Mad-Rat. "And where . . . where are my feathers?"

Before he could explain, she shushed him and led him to an old tuna can, into which he spat out the berries he'd been carrying in the pouches of his cheeks. When his mother looked into this tub, Montague had to support her.

"My colors," she said faintly. "All run together!"

"Oh, no, I'm terribly sorry!" His talking to the young she-rat had crushed all his mother's berries into a pulp.

"And . . . and what about my feathers?"

"You see, Mother, there was a fearful storm, and—"

"And all my feathers were lost! All!"

"We may as well put out the fires for now." One by one, Montague doused the fires beneath the dye vats. When this doleful task was completed, he tried to divert his mother with a colorful description of the storm. But she just dragged herself from vat to empty vat, staring into them forlornly. It made his heart ache to see her this way.

After a minute, he had an idea. "Isn't Aunt Elizabeth due in from Bermuda today, Mother? Let's go meet her. Come on. You could bring a—"

A hat to wave from the pier, he'd been about to say —but he caught himself, wisely avoiding the subject. His mother didn't look terribly enthusiastic, but she gave him her paw. And once they got away from her smoke and her hats, she perked up a bit.

They arrived at the pier to find it packed with humanity. Montague led his mother carefully around the edges of the mob and helped her with his tail up to the top of a piling at the tip of the dock. From here they had a panoramic view of a squad of tugboats pushing a tremendous ocean liner into the slip. The ship was tooting its whistles, and the water was polished gold by the late-afternoon sun, and all in all it was quite a festive atmosphere—except for the people.

When the ocean liner was tied to, the gangplank was lowered, and people in straw hats and loud Bermuda shorts poured off the ship, screaming to one another in earsplitting voices. The piling, however, was safely removed from all this. It was also convenient, for the stern line was cast there, and soon a solitary rat with a fancy French cigarette box on her back came tightrope-walking down that rope.

This was Aunt Elizabeth Mad-Rat. Although no longer young, Aunt Elizabeth was still a beautiful, exotic-looking she-rat, without a trace of white in her fur. Near the base of her tail, she wore a lovely silver ring worked with a design of suns and moons. On reaching the piling, she set down the French cigarette box, which was decorated with a picture of a dancing gypsy, and heaved a sigh.

"Your nose is brown as a berry, Liza," Mrs. Mad-Rat said encouragingly. "How was the cruise?"

"Oh, it was out of this world." Aunt Elizabeth looked wistfully back at the ocean liner. "The Bahamas ship doesn't leave till day after tomorrow."

Mrs. Mad-Rat sympathized. "But at least it will be nice for us to get to see you."

"It will be nice to see you, too. And I suppose Manhattan is an island of sorts, even though it never feels like one."

"Well, Liza, it's not one of your island paradises, certainly. But, as you say, it's an island of sorts."

"And here's Monty. Hello, Monty—*bonjour*."

"Hello, Aunt Elizabeth."

"You've gotten longer, Monty. Or at least your tail has. You're turning out to have quite a fine tail."

"Thank you, Aunt Elizabeth," he said, even though she'd told him exactly the same thing last month.

It was no easy matter prying Aunt Elizabeth away from the sight of the ocean liner. His aunt was mad for making life beautiful and exotic—in fact, Montague had heard that her love of cruises to faraway islands was the reason she'd left the mysterious uncle he'd been named after, Montague Mad-Rat the Elder. However, they finally managed to coax her off the pier and down into the gutter.

When they got home, the smoke had thinned out and the ratlings' screaming had died down to sleepy whimpers. Mr. Mad-Rat, still high on his slope, raised a paw in greeting before turning back to the battlements of his hundred and seventh castle. Mrs. Mad-Rat couldn't bear to light a fire with no decent berries in the house to melt down into dyes, so she set out a cold meal. While washing up, Montague examined himself in a cracked piece of mirror that leaned against the wall—a thing he never did. Wiping the

last drool stains from his snout, he inspected the growth of his fuzzy whiskers and the general shape of his head. He began to frown at his reflection. The longer he stared, the more certain he became that his ears were not quite the same size.

After dinner, Aunt Elizabeth advised him to open her cigarette box. There were no cigarettes in it, but it contained, among other things, two of the translucent golden seashells known as rat's halos.

"Thanks, Aunt Elizabeth," Montague said gratefully, examining them. "They're real beauties."

"Yes, you'll have a grand time working on those," she said. "May I see what you did with the last batch?"

The last batch consisted of two rat's halos she'd brought him back from a winter cruise in the Caribbean. He pulled open the drawer of a good-sized matchbox at the foot of his nestlike bed and brought out the two topmost shells.

"Oh, Monty, that's really lovely," Aunt Elizabeth said. "Such a beautiful sea-blue."

On the shell Aunt Elizabeth was staring at was painted a gardenia he'd found in Central Park, no doubt fallen from a human being's buttonhole, against a background of blue, his favorite color. It had taken him three months to complete. He painted the shells with the sharpened nib of a feather, tiny dot by tiny dot, using the strong, thick residue left at the bottom of his mother's dye vats. The other shell painting from that batch, of a butterfly wing he'd also found in the park, was only half finished.

"Yes," Aunt Elizabeth sighed, "splendid workmanship. You must have a grand collection by now, nearly a dozen, I'll bet."

"Thanks to you."

"Well, I try and do my best for you, Monty."

It was perfectly true. Aunt Elizabeth kept him well supplied with delicate golden canvases, and slow and difficult as the painting process was, he had always enjoyed it. Until the storm that afternoon, in fact, he had always assumed, along with his family, that painting seashells was the thing in life he was truly mad for.

Rats don't enjoy a favorable reputation among people, for certain rats nip and nibble in the night, and spread germs. Being so much less powerful than humankind, they were long ago forced underground —banished, in New York City at least, to dark, dreary gutters and basements. So a few decades ago, when the era of the great shipping lines came to a close and human commerce deserted a certain section of the city waterfront, a mass rat migration took place, most rats finding wharves infinitely preferable to drainpipes. The only wharf in the neglected strip which they failed to occupy was Wharf 51. A human being was living in Wharf 51, and rats in general have no more love for people than people have for rats. Mr. Pier-Person, as they called this human being, had invested all his money in buying up these particular wharves a month before they went out of business. Having sunk all his savings into it, Mr. Pier-Person was stuck living on his property. He turned very sour—and the rat invasion failed to cheer him up one bit.

The fastest, smartest rats, as it happened, moved into the wharves numbered in the sixties. These were the best. Having once served cargo ships, they were chock-full of empty crates that made luxurious single-family dwellings. But just as the rat families were getting used to their clean, comfortable new quarters, just as they were forming a government, Mr. Pier-Person began pushing a green wheelbarrow from wharf to wharf. The wheelbarrow was piled high with rat poison he'd gotten from the Board of Health —a cruel joke on the rats, as the poison was far from healthy. Many rats died horrible deaths. The rest had to choose between living in poisoned splendor or returning underground. For even if some rats were quite good-natured, they knew they would never conquer the human distaste for them.

But a shrewd rat among them came up with a plan against the Green Plague, as they called the wheelbarrow. Most rats are excellent scroungers and hoarders, with a particular fondness for shiny things like coins. Since Mr. Pier-Person's sourness resulted from the loss of all his money, which he groused about constantly, this shrewd rat suggested they give him a sort of rent. The rats pooled their secret hoards of money and went out into the streets to harvest more. On a midsummer night, when a long dry spell had emptied the giant rain barrel that stood outside Wharf 51, the rat population, which numbered in the millions, filled it nearly to the brim with their hoardings, fifty thousand dollars' worth of coins. So there would be no mistake as to where the money came from, they covered the top of the pile with a dozen of the poisoned corpses of their fellow rats. Like magic, the poisoning stopped the very next day; and every summer since that time they had refilled the rain barrel with fifty thousand dollars in coins scrounged from the city streets. Mr. Pier-Person had long since moved away into a high-rise apartment building, ridding them of their horrifying neighbor, and he allowed them to remain on his worthless wharves in peace.

In this strip of wharves, Wharf 62 was perhaps the grandest, and it was into this wharf that Isabel Moberly-Rat scurried after kissing Montague on the curb that afternoon of the summer storm. She favored the pint-sized dormouse with a smile, then wended her way to one of the largest crates, crate number 11, near the tip of the wharf. She slipped in by the back crack, hoping to avoid her mother, who was a bit excitable. But, as luck would have it, her mother was doing a petal arrangement in the kitchen, an activity Mrs. Moberly-Rat had taken up to keep her mind off cheese. Judging by her plumpness, however, this strategy hadn't been too successful.

"Mercy!" she exclaimed, dropping a rose petal. "Is that you, Izzy? You look like nothing on earth!"

"Oh, people," Isabel muttered under her breath. "There was this monstrous storm, Mother. You must have heard it."

Mrs. Moberly-Rat stated that Mrs. Reese-Rat had just sent her Ellie over with petals collected from underneath a flower stall—and Ellie had been on the same field trip as Isabel. "And she didn't look as if she'd been . . . dragged through the gutter!"

"Ellie didn't get blown off the bus," Isabel replied rather proudly. "Oh, and Mother, I lost my umbrella."

"Blown off the bus? Lost your umbrella? How under the sun did you get home? You didn't ride the bus alone, I hope!"

"Of course not." Isabel tugged off the soiled blue ribbon from around her neck and tossed it into the garbage, explaining that it was shot.

"Izzy, you didn't go down into the subway, did you?"

"No."

"Then . . . Mercy! You have a snoutbleed!"

Fortunately, rats only blush in their ears. Isabel quickly wiped her snout, which had picked up some berry juice from kissing Montague.

"Really, Izzy, you look like an old shoe. Here, have a bit of Muenster."

Isabel stamped a hind foot—not at the idea of Muenster cheese, but at the idea of looking like an old shoe. "Could I help it if a tidal wave knocked me into a gutter?"

"Gutter! Isabel Moberly-Rat! You might have a germ!"

Mrs. Moberly-Rat bustled off to siphon her daughter a bath in their ham tin—for they had cleverly run a tube from their crate up to a water tank on the roof of the wharf. Before long, Isabel was lying peacefully among the soap bubbles, daydreaming about her stormy adventures.

But it wasn't in her mother's nature to let her be. "What under the sun were you doing near a gutter in the first place?" Mrs. Moberly-Rat asked, sinking onto the flattened edge of the ham tin.

"It was under the *rain*, Mother," Isabel observed.

"But what were you doing there?"

"Well, to tell you the truth, I was having a conversation through the grate."

"Through the grate! Not with a stranger, I hope! But who do we know who takes the gutters?"

Isabel stirred the bubbles with a paw. Since migrating to the wharves, most rats had disowned their underground past. "Well, he was a stranger, I guess," she admitted. "But he introduced himself."

"He?"

"He was very nice, Mother—in a ridiculous sort of way. He absolutely saved my life with his tail."

"With his tail!" Mrs. Moberly-Rat cried hysterically, nearly slipping into the tub.

"Yes. I'm sure I'd have been swept off to the ends

of the earth if he hadn't thrown me his tail. He has quite a fine one, Mother."

"Isabel!"

"Well, he does."

"A stranger who throws his tail around! Really, Isabel, sometimes I think I'll have to ask your father to have a little talk with you. He *was* a wharf rat, wasn't he?"

"Of course."

"Well, thank goodness for small mercies. And you know this rat's name?"

"To tell you the truth, I'm not sure whether to believe him. He said his name was Montague Mad-Rat, but really, that's almost too funny, isn't it?"

Mrs. Moberly-Rat's hysteria vanished. She rose and stared down at her daughter.

"That's what he told me," Isabel said, blowing

some bubbles off her paw. "And he really was sweet. He sacrificed all his feathers for me."

"Isabel," her mother said gravely. "Haven't you ever heard of the Mad-Rats?"

"I don't think so. Why?"

"Why? Because they're notorious. They make things with their *own paws*. They marry their cousins. And one of them's said to have dealings with *people*."

Isabel sucked in her breath. Rats were supposed to collect money with their paws, not make things.

"And instead of a wharf," Mrs. Moberly-Rat went on, "they live in—well—in places I can't mention."

"Can't mention," Isabel whispered, awestruck. "But where's that?"

"I couldn't say. But it's a place I wouldn't wish on a common brown rat."

"Oh, *please* tell me! It's agony not to know! At least *spell* it, Mother—dearest, skinniest Mother!"

"Oh, all right. They're said to live in S-E-W-E-R-S."

"Sewers!" Isabel's snout wrinkled up. "But wouldn't that *smell*?"

"I don't say they're *active* sewers. But I'm sure the air's none too fresh."

"Ick," Isabel said primly. Most wharf rats, who live near water and know how to siphon, put a premium on cleanliness. To look like an old shoe was horrid, but to stink was unthinkable. Suddenly Isabel's ears pricked up. "Wasn't that a knock?"

"The groceries, probably. I do hope he remembered the Swiss. Oh, now, if you think you're going to make beady eyes at the delivery rat again, young lady, you're sadly mistaken. He's a common brown rat."

"But it might be Randal Reese-Rat!" Leaping out of the tub, Isabel shook herself dry in a flash. "Ellie said he might drop in to see me today."

"Oh, well, in that case. Let me get it, though. It'll be more seemly. Then I'll fix us all a snack."

But Isabel, who was light on her paws, slipped past her plump mother and scurried toward the front crack. On the way, she dashed into her room and tied a fresh blue ribbon around her neck, a little touch of her own of which she was rather proud.

The next afternoon, Montague collected double supplies for his mother. In spite of his berry-swollen cheeks and all the feathers looped in his tail, he stopped as he came out onto Columbus Circle and stared through the traffic at the place under the statue where he'd first seen the young Moberly-Rat yesterday. But if he lingered long, the berries would turn to mush in his mouth again, so he ducked into the grate without having glimpsed so much as a blue ribbon, and pattered homeward. How lonely it seemed, creeping along underground with no beady eyes to glance back at!

But at least his mother was pleased to see him.

"None crushed!" she cried ecstatically when he spat

the berries into the tuna can. "Liza, come see! Aren't they glorious?"

Aunt Elizabeth trudged over through the smoke, wiping her watery eyes. "Glorious," she said flatly.

In no time, Mrs. Mad-Rat was busy sorting berries by color and dumping them into her soup cans. She shuffled from vat to vat, stirring the contents, deaf to the ratlings' screams. But eventually she turned and said: "Really, Liza, it's only one more day before you shove off again."

"What?" Aunt Elizabeth grunted, awakening from a rat nap.

"That wasn't you sighing, dear? Why, Monty, what's the matter?"

Montague turned from his self-inspection in the piece of mirror. "Excuse me?"

"You were sighing, dear. You never sigh."

"Was I?"

"Preserve us! But don't worry, son—the juices'll be melted down pretty soon, and you'll be back at your butterfly before you know it. It's been a couple of days since you've had your paws in the paints, hasn't it?"

"I suppose," he said with another sigh.

"There! Didn't you hear that one?"

"Reminds me of Moony," Aunt Elizabeth remarked wistfully. "When I was leaving him, he used to sigh like crazy."

Montague perked up a bit. He'd always been curious about the uncle he'd been named after, whom his aunt called Moony. But his mother had warned him that Uncle Moony was a touchy subject and never to bring him up unless Aunt Elizabeth did so herself. "Why did you leave him, Aunt Elizabeth?" he asked, seizing this rare opportunity.

"Oh, well, Moony could be quite charming, but he lives in a sewer, too—under the Central Park Zoo, by a steam pipe, even smokier than this. He uses the steam pipe as a forge, you see, for doing up his rings. He's mad for doing up rings. But there weren't any . . . horizons down there. A rat needs horizons, Monty —at least, I do."

"Why doesn't he ever visit us?"

"Well, last time he dropped by, you were just a ratling, dear," Mrs. Mad-Rat explained. "He was drunk as a lord on dandelion wine, and he had a grimy sort of sidekick with him, a pack rat with the shiftiest eyes you ever saw. Heaven knows how Moony affords dandelion wine!"

"I'm afraid," Aunt Elizabeth confided, "that he's gotten himself mixed up with *people*. And to think I'm responsible!"

"Now, don't go blaming yourself, Liza dear. You know what they say. A rat's fate is always lying in wait."

"How is he involved with people?" Montague asked, wide-eyed.

"From what I gather," Aunt Elizabeth said, "this disreputable pack-rat character has some kind of hold over him. You know pack rats—go anywhere, mix with anyone, just so long as they keep their packs full. Born barterers. He has Moony doing his rings up for some person, it seems, and in return he keeps poor Moony supplied with his wine. I don't know the ins and outs of it, but it's not a pretty story."

"Why did you name me after him, Mother?" Montague asked.

"Well, dear, when we made you Moony's namesake, he and Aunt Elizabeth were still together, and he was still doing his rings up for *her*."

"I had more rings than I could squeeze onto my tail," Aunt Elizabeth said proudly, flashing her silver ring. "But this is the only one I kept, our wedding ring. You learn to travel light."

Montague, who'd always admired the ring, asked about the suns and moon phases that decorated it.

"Well," she said, "Moony used to swear he loved me more than the sun and moon."

Montague sighed again. If only he had such a ring to present to the young Moberly-Rat!

"Goodness, Monty," his mother declared, "you're not yourself at all! I'm afraid you overdid it in the park today. Take a little rat nap before dinner, why don't you?"

"I think I'll take a creep around."

"Well, if you like. But the dyes are thickening up."

Montague crept along the underground passageways and came up across the street from Wharf 62.

Crouching on the curb, staring at the grand wharf, he could all but feel the kiss that had been planted on his bulging cheek the day before. Was she inside that wharf now, or in some other strange and marvelous place of which he knew nothing? And wherever she was, what name did she go by? Possibilities had danced through his mind all day: Rosalind, Daphne, Sophia, Penelope . . . Rosalind seemed a nice name for a rat—but even that didn't quite do justice to her graceful creep, her bright laugh, her beady eyes.

An enormous truck rumbled up, and a human being got out and threw some fruits and vegetables in front of the wharf. How charitable, Montague thought. Perhaps human beings didn't deserve their terrible reputation, after all. The truck rolled on to the next wharf, and as time went by, Montague became indifferent to his surroundings. The sun fell below the river, and the air turned cooler, but he didn't notice. Nor did he notice the streetlamps flickering on, high up in the sky. His stomach growled, but he didn't hear it. An old, bent-over brown rat and his spouse circled him, staring, but he was unaware of them until the old brown he-rat poked him with his Popsicle-stick cane.

"Dead?"

Montague blinked at the elderly couple.

"Thought you were a stiff," the old brown rat apologized. "Poisoned or some such. Something give you a bad turn?"

Montague shook his head.

"Going to the Grand Rat Chat?" the brown rat asked.

"What's a Grand Rat Chat?"

"What's a Grand Rat Chat! Why, it's only the backbone of a democratsy! Hear that, Minerva? This one hasn't heard of Rat Chats—and him a wharf rat, too, by the size of him!"

"Sakes alive!" exclaimed the wife.

The old brown couple remained standing beside Montague on the curb, and eventually he asked if the Rat Chat was convening in the vicinity. The old he-rat informed him that it was being held in Battery Park, just below the financial district, but that his wife was bound and determined to get a close-up look at the leading wharf rats beforehand.

"Clarence Reese-Rat, you know, and Hugh Moberly-Rat. They both live in 62."

"Moberly-Rat!" Montague cried. "Who is he?"

"Who's Moberly-Rat! Why, where've you been, young sir?"

Montague sighed. "At home, mostly, and in the park," he admitted.

"Why, Hugh Moberly-Rat's one of the noblest rats around, a cabinet member and a great helper of ratkind."

The old brown wife squealed with delight as a group of elegantly groomed wharf rats emerged from the wharf across the street. "Look, Clarence's wife,

Lavinia!" she said. "And there's Clarence himself! And here come the Moberly-Rats! There's the missus —she's put on a little more weight, it looks like."

"Has the whole pack down cold," the husband whispered, nudging Montague. "Calls them by their first names."

"There's Hugh!" she shrieked. "See, how his tail twitches!"

Montague grabbed her paw. "But who's that?" he asked. "With the blue ribbon around her neck?"

"Blue ribbon? Why, Isabel, of course—Hugh's daughter. Quite a flair she has!"

"And that's her brother, taking her paw?"

"No, no. That's young Randal Reese-Rat."

"Oh," said Montague.

Isabel! he thought. How right that sounded! But soon Isabel was out of sight, led off on the forepaw of young Randal Reese-Rat, son of some prominent wharf rat. The old brown wife was tugging at her husband, and when Montague asked if he might ac-company them to the Grand Rat Chat, they said they would be honored.

Although Montague had always known that New York City was considered the rat center of the world, he was struck dumb by the number of rats gathered that evening in Battery Park. On a slope stretching back from a bench under a streetlamp were hundreds of rows of rats, with hundreds in each row, rats of every size and description, every shade of brown, gray, and black—over a million in all. Brown rats seemed to be mostly toward the back, at the top of the slope, so Montague crouched there with his new acquaintances. Thanks to the old brown rat's hobble, they were late, and a lady chair-rat, leaning over a dented beer can on the bench, was already introducing the first speaker, who was the Secretary of the Treasury. The Secretary, another wharf rat, took over the beer can and delivered a rousing little speech on the subject of the Rat Rent, for it was the time of summer for the annual collection of coins to fill the rain barrel. But not everything, it seemed, was as it had been in years past, and soon the Secretary surrendered the beer can to the lady chair-rat again.

"To acquaint you better with the new developments," she said, after thanking the Secretary, "I now, with the utmost sense of the honor heaped on me, perform my duty of introducing this evening's main speaker. But what can I tell you of this rat that you haven't already chewed over in your minds? He has received so many awards for his services to ratkind that I won't even attempt to name them. So, without further ado, I give you a great rat, a rat for all seasons —Hugh Moberly-Rat!"

As he took over the dented podium, Mr. Moberly-Rat acknowledged the noisy applause with a small bow, presenting a view of the top of his head, which was quite bald. He was unimpressive in stature, as was his tail, which twitched distractingly off to his left. But his voice was one of those screechy voices that rats find so thrilling, and his opening "My fellow rats!" sent a shiver of pleasure through the crowd.

"My fellow rats!" Mr. Moberly-Rat repeated, turning very solemn. "We live, I regret to say, in a more perilous age than any in the long history of ratdom. Ahem. We exist, I'm sorry to have to mention, in a more dangerous era than any in our glorious annals. How so, you ask? Why, you want to know? Quite simply, because of the staggering effectiveness—the ferocious efficiency—of the rat poisons perfected by our fellow citizens, the human beings."

The mention of human beings drew hisses from the crowd.

"Many of you have heard, I am fully—entirely—aware," Mr. Moberly-Rat went on, "that during this past week several unsuspecting rats have met horrible deaths—have, in short, crossed the terrible gulf. But there should be no one in the dark about this. Every rat should know. For more deaths, I fear, lurk in the near future—await us in the coming days. Their latest method of poisoning is cruel beyond telling or description. Poisons have been injected into fruits and vegetables, which have then been thrown at our doors like charity, cast under our very snouts in a cruel imitation of kindness. And soon, I daresay, even harsher measures may be resorted to. How so, you wonder—may *well* wonder. And what can be done about it? Answering these questions, my fellow rats, is the purpose, the pith, the sole object of this Grand Rat Chat."

"Any clues?" several rats shrieked from the crowd, as Montague recalled in horror the fruits and vegetables he'd seen scattered in front of Isabel's wharf.

"None," Mr. Moberly-Rat replied sadly. "Nary a one. Except that Mr. Pier-Person hasn't been sighted. No one, it seems, has laid eyes on him. Which is unusual, as he generally comes around at this time of the year to make sure the rain barrel's good and empty—ready and waiting for our offering, you might say. But this year a younger man—a more youthful type altogether—has been seen poking around. Maybe Pier-Person's getting too old to come himself. It could be the years are catching up with him. But that's the only clue. I wish to goodness I could enlighten you further, friends. I could almost wish, fellow rats, for a hat, so that I might pull the reason for the poisonings out of it. But rats don't wear hats. And alas, I'm a plain and simple cabinet minister, not a magician."

As thousands of rats exchanged anxious looks, Montague stared at the ground, feeling sick inside. How unspeakably ignorant he was! All these important things happening in the rat world, poisonings and Pier-Persons, and he'd never heard of any of them! And why? Because he spent all his time painting his silly seashells and collecting supplies for his mother to make hats, which rats never wore! How trivial his concerns seemed, compared to these earthshaking ones! For the first time, Montague began to realize that his life was dark and narrow and dreary.

It took a rather peculiar happenstance to make him lift up his eyes. In spite of the solemn nature of the occasion, laughter began to ripple through the crowd. A mangy old wharf rat was weaving his way around the front row toward a cardboard box on one side of the bench. Following him down the slope was a seedy, yellow-eyed pack rat with a marble sack on his back. Montague was sure he'd noticed that pack rat a few times, poking around in Central Park—and yet it was the leader of the odd pair that fascinated him. Mangy as he was, this rat bore a striking resemblance to Montague's father.

To the growing amusement of the crowd, the mangy rat huffed and puffed up the box onto the bench, where he weaved across and took over the beer can from a startled Mr. Moberly-Rat. When the hooting finally died down, the mangy rat cleared his throat to speak. But he couldn't seem to find his voice. He sniffed the top of the beer can. Taking it in both paws, he tilted it up. It was quite empty. The seedy pack rat crept nervously up to his side. Dropping the beer can, the mangy wharf rat reached into the sack on the pack rat's back and pulled out an eyedrop bottle. He unscrewed the dropper and squirted some golden liquid into his mouth.

"There," he pronounced. "Well now, sorry to butt in this way, but I thought I ought to put in my two cents' worth, seeing as a friend of mine's a human being and I heard him say—"

The rat world hissed—not only at the idea of a human being as a friend, but also at the rat's disappointing speaking voice, far less impressive and screechy than Mr. Moberly-Rat's. The hissing turned Montague's fascination to forboding.

"I just thought I ought to come forward, and so on," the mangy wharf rat continued once the hissing quieted down, "because just last Monday I happened to overhear Mr. Pick-Person talking into his telephone. 'I hear they're going to be exterminating some of those slummy wharves, dear.' That's what he said."

"Slummy?" cried a wharf rat. "Who said slummy?"

"Pier-Person?" yelled another. "You're a *friend* of Pier-Person?"

"*Pick*-Person," the mangy rat corrected. "Anyway, he was telling Mrs. Pick-Person—his mate, you know —how he hoped *I* didn't live in one of the wharves. Nice of him, wasn't it? He'd heard the old owner had died, you see, and the nephew was planning to sell them off for parking lots—and so on and so forth. Personally, I live very comfortably under the Central Park Zoo, but since most of you seem to cherish your wharves, I thought I ought to . . . and so forth."

"Slummy, indeed!" wharf rats protested. "Look who's calling *us* slummy!"

"You've got a human being for a *friend?*" others shrieked indignantly.

"He's a"—*hiccup*—"a business associate, really," the mangy wharf rat replied. "But that's a long story. Suffice it to say that I do some jewelry work for him, in a manner of speaking—decorating rings, and so forth and so on."

"Imagine, working with his paws!" the old brown he-rat said in a shocked undertone.

"Working with his paws!" his wife echoed, outraged.

"And him a wharf rat, too—though a poor excuse for one," her husband added. "Tipsy, by the look of him."

"I just *bet* it's Montague Mad-Rat!" the old brown she-rat said sharply. "I bet you a nickel!"

"Who's that?" her husband queried.

"Sakes alive!" she said irritably. "Haven't you heard of *anybody*? Why, Montague Mad-Rat's notorious—infamous! I bet even this youngster's heard of *him*. Right?"

But Montague only stared down the rat-ridden slope at the bench. As the boos and hisses grew louder, the sidekick pack rat nosedived off the back of the bench and vanished into the night. Trying to make himself heard once more, the mangy wharf rat—who was plainly Montague's Uncle Moony—had trouble clearing his throat again and looked around for his eyedropper. Finding the pack rat and his pack nowhere in sight, Uncle Moony shrugged and climbed down to the box. He paused there to catch his breath, then lowered himself to the ground and wove off into the night as well.

Meanwhile, Mr. Moberly-Rat and the lady chair-rat set the beer can to rights.

"Fellow rats, please!" Mr. Moberly-Rat's fine screech calmed the crowd. "We may not like human beings," the noble rat went on. "We may not care for them as a species—but we cannot ignore them. They're too big. Once before in our history, in the days of the Green Plague, we were threatened with extermination—menaced with wholesale slaughter. How did we win Mr. Pier-Person over then? How, on that glorious occasion, did we tug on his heartstrings? With hard currency, my fellow rats—with money. Money, my friends, is the language they understand. So what is our only chance with this new, this younger and more youthful Pier-Person?"

"Money?" tentative voices called from the crowd.

"Exactly!" Mr. Moberly-Rat replied. "Precisely! Being Mr. Pier-Person's nephew, he surely knows about the rain barrel. We'll just have to put in more money—more hard currency—twice as much."

A million rats sucked in their breath in dismay.

"What else can we do?" Mr. Moberly-Rat screeched. "What other recourse do we have? Let's consider it a challenge. Let's consider it a cry to all decent rats to buckle down to their duty of scouring the streets and sidewalks for change. R.R.R., we could call it: Raising the Rat Rent. And let me be the first to tell you, in the plainest language possible, that there isn't a moment to lose. Every second wasted from here on in is a second lost, down the drain, a forsaken opportunity, a missed chance. And so let's see if we can't raise this year's hundred thousand dollars right *now*—tonight— this very evening! If you didn't bring a whole dime, give a nickel. If you can't give a nickel, at least give a penny. Our welfare depends on it. All that we rats hold dear hangs in the balance. Life as we know it . . ."

Mutters of grudging agreement swept the great assembly. Many of the rats had brought flip-top cigarette boxes and other containers, and the old brown she-rat, who was clutching a book of matches under a paw, now opened it and pulled a nickel proudly from behind the rows of matches.

"No pennies, young sir?" she asked, giving her coin a shine on her fur.

Montague turned away without replying.

"Oh, now don't go creeping off with your snout hanging down and your tail between your legs!" the old brown he-rat said, waving him back with his Popsicle stick. "It's not such a crime to be poor."

But Montague felt too ashamed even to look back— and not just because he was poor.

Montague scuttled off through the dark, empty alleyways of the financial district. The mystery that had haunted him was finally solved: the other young rats in the park had laughed at him, even with no feathers looped in his tail, even with no berries bulging his cheeks, because he had introduced himself to them. His name, Montague Mad-Rat, was notorious throughout the rat world. Why hadn't he known the dreadful truth about his uncle earlier? And why had he been left to learn from strangers that it was degrading to make things with one's own paws rather than scouring the streets for money? As he crept along a curbstone, he kept his eyes peeled for coins, but although he'd happened upon them often enough in the park, when he hadn't cared about them, he didn't see so much as a penny tonight. Finally, he slipped through a grating and started homeward along a winding drainpipe still damp from yesterday's storm. But his creep grew mopish, and after a while he stopped in a crouch, brooding.

The worst thing of all was that he'd told his name to Isabel. Of all rats, why had his parents had to name him after that mangy uncle of his? If only he'd been smart enough to tell Isabel that he was a different rat! Oh, if only he *were* a different rat, not a Mad-Rat at all! But no doubt Isabel hadn't given him a thought since yesterday. And now she was probably perched under that bench in a reserved front-row place beside young Randal Reese-Rat, listening to her famous father.

When Montague had been brooding for some time, a strange sound came echoing down the pipe. As it grew louder, he realized it was a rat, singing. It seemed to be quite a pretty song. Before long, he made out the words.

> *Rings are round the sun and moon,*
> *And inside of trees;*
> *Some are made by angel rats,*
> *Some in factories.*

> *Some rings hoop around the heart,*
> *From a lover, or a friend;*
> *But all are circles—none begin,*
> *And none will ever end.*

The sweetness of it lifted Montague's spirits in spite of himself, and a smile flickered across his snout. But when the singer rounded a bend in the pipe, the smile departed. It was none other than his infamous uncle.

The mangy rat stopped singing at the sight of him. "Seen a pack rat come by here, clinking?" he asked.

Montague shrank back in horror and disgust.

"What, is my breath winy?" his uncle asked, blinking and squinting in the dimness. "You know, you remind me of a rat I know, or something or other. What's your name?"

"The worst name in all ratdom," Montague said coldly. And, turning tail, he scampered off down the pipe.

When he got home, no one scolded him for missing dinner. No one even noticed him. Aunt Elizabeth and the ratlings were asleep. His mother was busy making feather hats with her paws, while his father was constructing mud castle number one hundred and seven with *his* paws. Montague's dinner had been left out, but he crept into his nest of a bed without taking so much as a nibble. To separate himself from his family, who appeared to him in a whole new light, he built a tent over himself with his covers, using his tail as the pole.

Long before morning, Montague's tail wilted and he fell asleep. He was awakened by Aunt Elizabeth singing brightly to his mother:

Sailing, sailing,
Over the bounding main.
Many a hat,
From many a vat,
'Ere you see me again!

This wasn't strictly true, as Aunt Elizabeth's Bahamas cruise was a short one, but still her high spirits were contagious. Montague got out of bed and studied his face in the mirror again. Then he told his mother he might go for a creep.

"Preserve us!" Mrs. Mad-Rat said. "You sigh, you

stare at yourself, last night you even miss dinner, and now you want to miss breakfast!"

"I only want to go out," he said, "and look for money for R.R.R."

"R.R.R.? What on earth is that?"

"Raising the Rat Rent, Mother."

"You hear that, Liza? Monty's going in for a cause!"

But Aunt Elizabeth was busy packing her fancy French cigarette box. Montague frowned.

"You're not really worked up about it, are you, Monty?" Mrs. Mad-Rat asked.

Montague pursed his snout. The truth was that the cause itself had managed to slip somewhat out of his mind overnight. However, finding a contribution would give him an excuse to visit Mr. Hugh Moberly-Rat, and if he was visiting the Moberly-Rats, he might catch a glimpse of Isabel.

"It's a noble cause, Mother."

"But, Monty, where do you suppose you'll find money?"

"In the streets, I guess, like other rats."

"But, dear, money's so dull. If you want to give to a noble cause, why not give something noble like . . ." Her eyes roamed over the feathered rat hats on the wall, but although none had ever been put to use—any more than anyone had ever lived in one of his father's mud castles—she winced at the thought of parting with a single hat. "Something like one of your lovely shells. His seashells are lovely, aren't they, Liza?"

"Yes," Aunt Elizabeth replied, glancing up, "soon I'll be at sea again. *Au revoir!*"

Montague considered the matchbox by the foot of his bed. "Do you really think they're better than money, Mother?"

"Of course," she replied easily. "Each of your shells is painted differently and each is quite breathtaking. In that respect, they're rather like . . ." Again, her eyes wandered to the feathered hats. "Naturally, they're better than money. Coins and bills all look pretty much the same."

This made a certain amount of sense. He gave his mother a hug and promised her double supplies on his next collecting day.

"Liza has to go in a couple of hours," she said, smiling. "Won't you come see her off?"

Of course he would. In the meantime, he worked on his butterfly painting. He gnawed the end of a fresh feather to a needle-like nib and dipped it into the thick midnight-blue residue left in one of his mother's vats. The only way to create a bright surface on the shell without globbing the heavy dye was to apply it in the tiniest imaginable dots and let each one dry before applying the next. By the time Aunt Elizabeth called out *"Au revoir"* to his father, he'd added only a minuscule part of the "eye" pattern on the wing.

Putting aside his feather, Montague hoisted his aunt's cigarette box onto his back and followed her and his mother down the smoky pipe. At the pier piling, his aunt took her luggage and tightrope-walked the stern line, the beautiful silver ring on her happily waving tail flashing in the sun. After shrieking a last *"Bon voyage!"* he walked his mother back to the sewer. Then he set off on his creep with his matchbox full of shells.

When Montague arrived at Wharf 62, the straight-backed little sentinel didn't recognize him at first.

"Yeeeees?" the dormouse inquired, eyeing the matchbox on Montague's back suspiciously.

"I'd like to see Mr. Hugh Moberly-Rat, please," Montague said.

"*You* want to see Mr. Hugh Moberly-Rat?"

"Yes, please."

"Haven't I . . . Aren't you the rat who's not even sure who he is?"

"I suppose so," Montague admitted.

The dormouse, pulling himself up to his fullest height—which still wasn't much—looked highly skeptical. "Is Mr. Moberly-Rat expecting you?"

"No. But, you see, I've come to give a contribution to R.R.R."

"Oh!" The dormouse stared again at the matchbox. "You don't mean to say that's full of . . ."

Montague nodded solemnly.

"Oh!" exclaimed the dormouse, suddenly giving a bow. "And here I took you for a firebug! Allow me to show you the way, sir."

It was very different from his first visit. The dormouse ushered him down the wharf, half-turning every few steps to execute another neat bow, and at the end of the wharf pointed out the crate numbered 11. Montague thanked him and knocked.

In a moment, a young she-rat with a blue ribbon around her neck appeared in the crack. "Hi," she said with a polite smile.

Montague stood there speechless. Could it really be that Isabel was only six inches away, smiling at him cordially? Yet there—looking inquisitively into his—were her beady gray eyes, even beadier and grayer than he remembered.

"Delivery?" she asked, looking at the matchbox.

"R.R.R." was all he could manage to say.

"Oh, a contributor! Come on in. Father's in his study."

He stepped in and followed her down the corridor. Unlike his sewer pipe, the crate was divided into rooms. Also unlike the sewer pipe, which was filled with the products of his parents' paws, the crate was furnished exclusively with exotic, people-made things, from wondrous luxuries like a ham-tin bathtub in an alcove to commemorative postage stamps on the walls. The hallway was tiled with bits of cork from inside bottle caps, so his tread hardly made a sound. He gawked at everything with deep admiration.

"Daddy!" Isabel called out as they approached a doorway at the end of the hall. "Here's a contributor."

"Show him in!" came a fine screech.

After pointing the way, Isabel trotted off, leaving Montague to stare after her. She hadn't even recognized him! Was it because his cheeks weren't pouched out with berries, or had she simply forgotten his existence?

"Come in!" came a curt screech. "Enter."

Montague entered the study obediently. The walls, papered with silver-foil gum wrappers, made him blink in amazement. Mr. Moberly-Rat was seated behind a huge dictionary with gilt-edged pages.

"Sorry if I sounded a little sharp—a trifle brusque," Mr. Moberly-Rat said, rising to extend a paw across the book. "I've been studying the figures from last night . . . Hugh Moberly-Rat. Please call me Hugh."

"Please call me Montague," Montague said, shaking the famous rat's paw.

"Montague, eh. You've got a good, firm shake. Have a seat, Montague. Take a pew."

Following Mr. Moberly-Rat's lead, Montague sat on a pinless satin pincushion by the book, holding the matchbox in his lap.

"Did you make it to the Rat Chat last night?" Mr. Moberly-Rat asked. "Did you attend?"

"Yes, indeed, sir. And I'm sure your appeal gnawed at everyone's mind."

"Well, thank you, Montague, thank you. That's very kind of you—most considerate. I can only wish it had gnawed a little more at their purse strings."

"Sir?"

"The figures, Montague—these tabulations. Tragic. Deeply disappointing. All those rats, and barely the usual fifty thousand dollars. A dime apiece would have done it. Time is the thing. It's of the essence, you might say. Of course, if Pier-Person's nephew could wait a year—till next summer—we could probably double our usual payment without the least, the slightest difficulty. But we need it right now! We require it this instant! Still, I must say, it's cheering to see a rat who comes back to give more."

Montague fidgeted on his cushion. "But you see, sir, I had nothing to give last night."

"Oh?" Mr. Moberly-Rat smiled at the matchbox. "So you brought us some real money today, Montague? Some hard currency?"

"No, sir. Something better."

"Better!" Mr. Moberly-Rat exclaimed in his finest screech. "Superior to money? Good heavens—what?" He leaned forward across the dictionary to get a good look as Montague pulled open the drawer of the matchbox.

"Here's one," Montague said shyly, setting on the book the shell with the gardenia painted on a field of blue.

Mr. Moberly-Rat stared. "What in the name of heaven is this?"

"A rat's halo, sir. A painted seashell."

"A seashell? A shell from the sea, you mean?" The

great rat narrowed his eyes at him. "What is this? Have you been into ratnip?"

"No, sir. But I've done others, if you don't care for that one. Each one is different, and both my mother and Aunt Elizabeth think they're quite lovely."

"Your mother and Aunt Elizabeth! Rat's halos!" Mr. Moberly-Rat's tail began to twitch off to the left. "What kind of wharf rat are you, anyway? What did you say your name was?"

"Montague, sir."

"Montague what?"

Montague knew better now than to divulge his family name. But he'd had little practice at lying, having spent so little time in society, and for a moment he just sat there in foolish silence. Suddenly the great rat's jaw fell open. Too late, Montague remembered that he signed all his shells.

"Mad-Rat!" Mr. Moberly-Rat whispered.

The great rat's paw jerked away from the shell as if it were covered with slime. But ever so gradually his look of horror turned to one of understanding. He nodded slowly. He smiled.

"Well, Montague Mad-Rat," he said graciously, rising and coming around the gilt-paged book. "I'm awfully glad you stopped by—terribly! Tickled pink!"

Mr. Moberly-Rat called for his daughter and herded Montague out of the silver-foiled study. Soon Isabel floated breezily down the corridor.

"Izzy, please show our friend Mr. Mad-Rat out,"

Mr. Moberly-Rat said. "Splendid to see you, Mr. Mad-Rat. Truly splendid—genuinely delighted!" And with a final cordial smile Mr. Moberly-Rat turned back to his figures, leaving Montague in total bewilderment.

"Mad-Rat?" Isabel said, staring. "But you're not the . . . You couldn't be the . . . But what happened to your cheeks? No more berries?"

"No," Montague replied in a daze.

"But your voice," Isabel said. "It's changed, too. It's much nicer. Same reason?"

"I suppose."

She led him to the front crack. He stepped through but turned with his tail still inside the crate. He couldn't take his eyes off her.

"Is my bow crooked, or what?" she finally asked.

"Oh, no, it's perfect! I've never seen a rat with a bow before."

She smiled. "What is it, then?"

"Oh . . . nothing," he said. "Isabel?"

"That's me. And you're Montague, right? But do tell me something, since you're here. Is it true you live in a . . . S-E-W-E-R?"

"I suppose so," he said, even more bewildered.

"I'll be! And after the Rat Chat last night everyone was saying . . . Was that your father who was so . . . so tipsy?"

"My uncle," he said, hanging his head. "But I don't even know him."

"Hmmm."

"But . . ." He lifted his eyes. "Isabel?"

"Montague?" she said, her snout quivering.

"Oh . . . nothing."

"Why," she cried, breaking down at last into her bright laughter, "you're almost as mad as your uncle, aren't you?"

Her laughter got the better of her so completely that her ears actually blushed—and he turned away and crept down the wharf. But before he'd taken many steps, the sound of his name made him glance back over his shoulder.

"Didn't you forget your box?" Isabel asked, her pretty head poking out of number 11.

He thought of the matchbox, filled with the worthless products of his own paws.

"You can throw it away," he said.

The dormouse's respectful bow was wasted on Montague as he scurried out of Wharf 62. All he wanted just now was *not* to be noticed—to disappear. He dove into the drainpipe and headed for Central Park, for a secluded spot where he sometimes took a break from his feather and berry hunting.

Since the storm, the weather had been fresh and light, and this afternoon the various creatures in the park were all astir, playing in the sunshine or gathering nuts in the shade or, in the case of many young human beings, swooshing along at fur-raising speeds on bicycles or roller skates. But once Montague reached his hiding place, under a laurel bush on the bank of the great reservoir, he hardly budged an inch. He crouched in the shadow staring out at the ruffled waters until he remembered that one of his shells bore a picture of this view, painstakingly created from memory. He turned his tail to the reservoir. Soon the mere sight of the forepaws with which he'd painted his shells grew hateful to him, and he tucked them under his body. There wasn't a hint of moisture in the air today, but his fur ended up getting wet anyway, for he felt so hopeless that tears began to run down his snout.

After about a dozen tears, however, Montague wiped a paw across his face. There must be a way to see Isabel again—there just had to be. He thought of all the times he'd come across pennies and nickels in the park before he'd learned the value of money— sometimes even quarters and subway tokens. He would scour the park: that was what he would do. And when he'd collected enough to fill a whole ciga- rette box, he would drag it back to Wharf 62.

Montague crept down to the bridle path that encir- cled the reservoir. Soon he made his first find: a penny half buried in the cinders on the edge of the path. He lugged it back to his bush, hid it under some dead leaves, and sallied forth again, daydreaming of Isabel and of helping in his small way to save the wharf where she lived. The truth is, it's nearly impossible for healthy young rats to remain hopeless for more than about an hour.

While Montague was setting out on his treasure hunt in Central Park, the Moberly-Rats had another visitor at crate 11. This was young Randal Reese-Rat, who lived with his well-to-do family in crate number 8 on the same wharf. Although his tail was a bit on the scrawny side, Randal was a handsome young rat. His fur was always perfectly in place, never ratted, and he always smelled good. A year ago, he had purchased a sample of men's cologne from a pack rat, who'd snitched it out of a postman's sack, and ever since Randal had worn a dash behind his ears. He also yawned a lot for his age. He looked down his snout at rats who were too wide awake, too enthusiastic or emotional. But today he was so very pleased with himself that he had to fight back a foolish grin of his own when Isabel greeted him. It required a real effort just to look at her droopily and pay a casual compliment on her ribbon.

Usually, Randal traveled with a toothbrush for touching up his fur when he came in out of the wind, but today he was carrying instead the box the cologne bottle had come in. When Isabel showed him into the living room, he opened the box and pulled out a wad of green paper.

"Found that this morning," he remarked, tossing the green wad carelessly on the pile of magazines that served as a coffee table.

Isabel unfolded the wad. "A dollar!" she marveled. "Oh, Randal, wherever did you find it?"

"Human construction site, down near the mouth of the great tunnel," Randal replied, stifling a yawn. "Saw it fall out of one of their pockets."

"Gad! How'd you get it?"

"Well, it wasn't easy, if I do say so myself. I had to wait around for ages. It was a real bore." He gave way to a yawn. "The worst of it was, I had to hide behind a pile of *dirt*."

"Ick!"

"And on my way back, out in front of the wharf, I got my *tail* wet, if you can imagine anything so tiresome. There's a human being spraying down the street."

"Oh, Randal, I hope you won't catch cold."

He sighed. "That's all I'd need. But anyway, my father's not home, and I thought maybe yours could give me change for the bill."

"A whole dollar," Isabel said thoughtfully. "Well, we could ask."

She led the way to the back of the crate. Her father, seated at the gilt-paged dictionary in the silvery study, was still looking rather annoyed from his last visitor, but he perked up considerably at the sight of the dollar bill. Although coins, with their glitter, cast a natural spell over most rats and were the usual currency when bartering for goods with pack rats, Mr. Moberly-Rat had enough experience in dealing with the annual Rat Rent to prefer paper money. He came around the book and congratulated Randal warmly on the rare find. Then he opened a candy box, which contained something better than candy, and after putting in the paper dollar, pulled out change: two quarters, three shiny dimes, and four nickels.

"Can you manage all that?" he asked. "Will it be too heavy for you?"

"Not if I leave you these, sir," Randal said magnanimously, setting a quarter and a nickel on the dictionary. "That's for R.R.R."

"Thirty cents!" Mr. Moberly-Rat whistled. "That's very generous of you, Randal, my boy—most liberal. Though I guess you're not really a boy anymore, are you? Boyhood, I suppose, is something you've left in the dust. You're a full-grown rat."

"I guess I am," Randal said modestly, casting a sidelong glance at Isabel.

"And a resourceful rat, too," Mr. Moberly-Rat went on, looking not at all displeased to see Randal take Isabel's paw. "A rat of means and ingenuity. If only there were more young rats like you! If only other rats of your generation were cut from the same cloth! Then I don't doubt doubling our payment would be easy as mouse pie. Then, I daresay, meeting this crisis would be as simple as—"

Isabel screeched. "Randal! Your tail!"

Dropping her paw, Randal lifted up his skinny tail. He dropped it as if it were a poisonous snake. The fine gray color drained out of his ears. "What *is* it?" he whispered, trembling.

Mr. Moberly-Rat rushed to his side and examined the tail. "Been near any rat poison?" he demanded, seeing the green splotch.

"Rat poison!" Randal shrieked, stumbling backwards.

Isabel reached too late to keep him from falling. He tripped over a curious thing, a seashell with a gardenia painted on it, and landed sprawled out on the matchbox left by the last visitor. Randal's shriek soon brought Mrs. Moberly-Rat bustling in. At the sight of his tail, she threw her forepaws in the air, dropping a chunk of blue cheese on the floor, and gave a piercing scream. Then she bustled out again to fetch a doctor.

"The human being spraying the streets," Randal said faintly, staring up terror-struck at Isabel and her father. "It's poison . . . They've killed me, nipped me in the bud."

"Spraying the streets!" Mr. Moberly-Rat exclaimed. "Good heavens, that means he may be doing the wharves by tomorrow! Within twenty-four hours, he could be contaminating our homes!"

"But what difference does it make?" Randal shrieked. "I'm dead already!"

Soon Mrs. Moberly-Rat burst in with a doctor and Mrs. Reese-Rat in tow. They carried Randal off to the guest bedroom, and the doctor, a general ratitioner, applied a poultice to the poisoned tail. After giving the young rat a piece of a pill pilfered from a pharmacy, the doctor ushered the rest of them out of the sickroom.

"It may keep the infection from spreading, it may not," whispered the doctor, who was never quite sure which pills were for what. "But, with any luck, it'll put him to sleep."

Before they could all creep away, Randal's voice rose feebly from within. His tearful mother started to go to him, but when Randal's voice rose again, it became clear that he was calling for Isabel.

Isabel went solemnly back into the guest room. As she approached the bedroom slipper in which the patient was lying, Randal's eyes flickered open weakly.

"Izzy, you're so beautiful in that blue ribbon . . . and your fur's so clean and shiny, with that bubble-bath scent," he said, sniffing faintly. "You're just like a dream."

"Oh, Randal, you have to rest now," she said with a crack in her voice. "Then you'll get better."

"Will I? Give me something to get better for, Izzy. Promise you'll be my wife, if I ever creep again."

"But, Randal, I'm so young!" she exclaimed, delighted.

"Ah, but promise you'll be true to me."

"I'll be true to you," she vowed fervently, taking the paw he'd put outside the covers. "Just as long as you want me."

"Thank you, Izzy," he said, yawning for once in earnest. "You're just like a dream . . . Who can say, maybe you are a dream . . ."

Then his eyes closed, and he drifted away from her.

The rest of the household was in a frenzy—Mrs. Reese-Rat and Mrs. Moberly-Rat over Randal's collapse, Mr. Moberly-Rat over the news that a human being, no doubt Mr. Pier-Person's nephew, was now spraying rat poison in the waterfront street. But Isabel, after leaving the patient, ducked into her room and twirled in front of the hand mirror propped against the wall. "Izzy, you're so beautiful in that blue ribbon," she whispered dreamily. "You're just like—"

Her father's screech interrupted her raptures. He wanted someone to fetch the dormouse. "I'm calling an emergency session of the cabinet," his voice rang in the hallway, "and I want him to clear out my study!"

Isabel stopped twirling and stepped into the corridor. "He's got enough to do, Daddy," she suggested, "and besides, he's so pathetically small, in spite of his posture. I'll move the junk out of your way."

"That's very considerate of you, Izzy," Mr. Moberly-Rat said, looking at her in considerable surprise. "Are you feeling all right? You didn't get any of that poison on you, did you?"

Shaking her head, she bounced into the study ahead of him. She placed the loose seashell on top of the matchbox and carted the load back to her room. There she propped the gardenia painting up beside the mirror. A funny thing happened then. As a rule, her own reflection had an irresistible fascination for her, but once she'd propped up the shell painting, her eyes didn't wander to the mirror once. After a while, she eased open the matchbox drawer. To her delight, there was a whole stack of painted seashells inside, nine more of them, making ten in all. One was of an oak leaf, another of a purple crocus, another a view of the reservoir in the park. Each seemed to her as extraordinarily beautiful as the last—even, unbelievably enough, one of a human child flying a kite. She leaned the shells all around the walls of her room and, crouching in the middle, turned in a slow circle, looking from one to the next. The overwhelming beauty made her feel tipsy, like the mangy Mad-Rat who'd spoken at the Grand Rat Chat.

Suddenly something that peculiar rat had said popped into her mind, something about doing business with a human being—business involving decorating rings. Didn't "business" usually mean money? And wasn't it possible that someone who paid for ring decorating might also pay well for these gorgeous shells? Of course, the "someone" was human, so the whole idea was as bizarre as it was scary. But still, the very thought of getting a lot of money inspired glorious images of herself as the heroine of R.R.R.

Under the Central Park Zoo, the mangy old rat had said he lived. Isabel, all excited, repacked the shells in a trice. After putting on a fresh ribbon, she carried the matchbox out to the front crack.

"Hello, Mr. Reese-Rat," she said, meeting that dignitary in the doorway.

"Ah, Clarence, come in, come in," Mr. Moberly-Rat added, shuffling toward them down the corridor. "Izzy, where do you think you're going?"

"Out," she replied.

"Oh, no, you're not, young lady. No rats are allowed out while that person's spraying the street. No one's to set a paw outside the wharf while young Pier-Person's out there poisoning the pavement."

"I'll use the gutters," Isabel said slyly.

"The gutters!" exclaimed Mr. Clarence Reese-Rat, who brought a hint of his son's cologne into the crate. "You will have your little joke, won't you, Isabel— even when the world's caving in around our ears!"

From the hall, Isabel could see into the living room, where her mother was trying to comfort Mrs. Reese-Rat with a selection of hard and soft cheeses. Once Mr.

Reese-Rat had peeked in sadly at his unconscious son, he and Mr. Moberly-Rat adjourned to the study. Isabel lugged the matchbox into the kitchen and slipped easily out the back crack.

The dormouse was missing from his post—perhaps because of the spraying just outside. A tank truck with a skull and crossbones on the side was parked by the curb, and a young man with a pinched face was showering the pavement with a hose plugged into the tank. But thanks to her experience with Montague, Isabel was not above lowering herself through a handy grate into an underground drainpipe. This, however, proved

a tricky operation. The seashells were too delicate to risk dropping.

She finally managed it—only to find that the drain was quite filthy. The underground stream from the last rainstorm had dried up, leaving a film of dirt, and since she had to carry the matchbox on her back, the ends of the fresh ribbon *would* drag along.

"Second one shot this week," she muttered.

Isabel's sense of direction was quite good, at least compared with her mother's, but on the way to the Central Park Zoo she had to keep squeezing up through gratings to look for familiar landmarks. By the time she shimmied up through the grate on Columbus Circle, the one she'd been swept into the day before yesterday, her fur was every which way. Someone she knew might be in the park, so she lowered herself back down and continued along underground, following a curvy pipe under one of the winding park roads.

The next time Isabel poked her head up, it was through a drain in the middle of a huge, outdoor cage. Resting on the other side of the drain was the largest snout she had ever seen. The snout belonged to a creature so colossal that, if it hadn't been furry, it would have been just as terrifying as a human being.

Isabel cleared her throat, ready to pop back down in a second. "Excuse me," she said. "Who are you?"

"Gr-r-r-r-retchen," the creature growled.

"Gretchen?" Isabel was rather surprised that the creature was a she. "Gretchen what?"

"Bear-r-r-r."

"Oh, thank you," Isabel said, deciding this most likely was the zoo.

Ducking back underground, Isabel explored numerous pipes, both concrete and iron. Finally, her nose told her that she was in the vicinity of other rats, but as she started down a wide, rather rusty steel pipe, the air grew hot and steamy. Her ribbon, already soiled, began to wilt, and she turned back.

Then a song wafted out of the steam.

> *Dawn is a ratling,*
> *Blind and screaming.*
> *Morning sets*
> *The mind to dreaming.*

Gold shall fill
The afternoon.
Yet silver's sweeter,
Sings the moon.

But, rats! Beware
That moony beaming.
Night is a grownup,
Blind and screaming.

It was a queer little song, but Isabel was drawn to it, and she only had to creep a bit farther down the vaporous pipe to find the source. It sounded like a love song, but it must have been a work song, for the singer was bent over a steam pipe, toiling away—with his paws! The same mangy rat who'd taken over the beer can from her father last night. And yet, somehow, the way the rat's voice, so ill suited to speechmaking, tenderly caressed the lyrics of the song made him look less mangy to her. After removing a large ring of gold from the smoking pipe with a pair of tweezers, he picked up a needle and began to etch a fine design in the gold. Squinting, he worked swiftly and precisely, while the gold was still soft and warm. Soon the ring was covered with clusters of leaves and flowers.

"That's lovely!" she couldn't help remarking, for the etched flower petals were more beautiful than any of her mother's arrangements.

The mangy rat turned and squinted at her. "So are you," he said.

She perched on her matchbox and tried to smooth out her fur. "I know you're Montague Mad-Rat's uncle," she told him. "I'm Isabel Moberly-Rat."

She was used to having this make an immediate impression, but he simply looked a little sad and said softly, "Montague's uncle." After a minute he added: "Care for a nip of wine? Pem!"

A yellow-eyed rat came sidling out of the smoke, carrying an eyedrop bottle half full of dandelion wine. This rat, Mr. Mad-Rat told her, was Pembroke Pack-Rat, his "business associate," but neither the pack rat's shifty eyes nor the wine he offered appealed to Isabel in the least.

"Superior vintage, this one, sir," the pack rat said, pulling out the dropper for the wharf rat.

"Ah, thanks, Pem."

Judging by the increased activity of his tail, Mr. Mad-Rat agreed with the pack rat's judgment of the vintage. Something silver flashed through the mangy fur at the base of his tail. It was, Isabel noticed, another ring, far smaller but of even finer workmanship than the gold one he'd just finished.

"How gorgeous!" she said, staring. "What's on it, the phases of the moon?"

"Mmm," he said. "The eye was sharper then, and the paw was steadier. It's moons, and suns—my wedding ring."

Pembroke Pack-Rat's eyes, fixing on the same silver ring, took on an almost greenish tint. Then his eyes shifted to her matchbox. "Empty?" he wondered.

"Mmm," Mr. Mad-Rat said, not seeming to realize the pack rat meant the matchbox. "I *was* feeling a bit empty, Pem. Liza must be sailing away on a ship—I can always feel it in my bones."

"Ah, yes, sir, that's natural," the pack rat sympathized. "And that there box? Empty, too?"

"Box, Pem? What box?"

"I was addressing the young lady rat, yer honor."

Isabel got off her seat. "It's painted seashells," she said, addressing Mr. Mad-Rat. "Your nephew did them, but he left them at our house. I was wondering about this beautiful work you do." She pointed at the etched ring. "Does this human being you know pay you in money?"

"Partly," Mr. Mad-Rat replied.

"Really!" Isabel exclaimed, pleased. "I wonder, then, since this person likes pretty rings, and since the poisoning's gotten so bad that my . . . my boyfriend Randal is on the brink of death with a tail infection . . ." In spite of the seriousness of the situation, she felt a thrill at using the words "my boyfriend." "I was wondering if maybe you could try and sell these paintings to your human being for money to help double the Rat Rent."

"Double the Rat Rent?" said Mr. Mad-Rat.

"Daddy hopes that may stop the poisoning," Isabel explained.

"Ah, I see."

While they were talking, the pack rat had nosed open the drawer of the matchbox and withdrawn the top shell, the one with the gardenia on it.

"Nice merchandise," Pembroke commented. "Fine workmanship."

"Fine workmanship!" Isabel hooted. "Why, it's better than that, it's art!"

Her indignation took even her by surprise; but Mr. Mad-Rat, screwing up his eyes, was quick to agree.

"A real Mad-Rat," he murmured with a trace of pride. "How do you happen to know Montague, Miss . . . What is it?"

"Moberly-Rat," she said, a little haughtily. "Isabel Moberly-Rat."

"Moperly-Rat," he said. "Well, Miss Moperly-Rat, you may have something there, in a manner of speaking. Wouldn't you think we might be able to sell 'em, Pem?"

"Could be, sir," said the pack rat, who was shuffling through the other shells. "They ain't none too sturdy, but the work's fine as fine."

"We could take 'em in on Monday, along with the rings, and see what Pick-Person has to say, and so on."

"Monday!" Isabel cried, forgetting her annoyance at the mispronunciation of her name. "But by Monday every wharf in the city could be poisoned!"

"But we always go Monday. Once we went on a Tuesday, but Mr. Pick-Person wasn't alone, his associates were in the gallery, so we couldn't transact. Once we went on a Wednesday, but he wasn't alone then either. What's today, Pem?"

"Thursday, yer honor."

"Mmm, and once we went on a Thursday, but that was no good for transacting either—and so on. He's the only person we deal with, you see."

"But it has to be today!" Isabel insisted.

"Surely you're exaggerating, Miss Moppery-Rat. The rat you're in love with is ailing, so you're all in a tizzy. Love's like that."

"I'm *not* in a tizzy!" Isabel declared indignantly, finding this the last straw.

"Ah. Then I pity poor Crandal."

"It's Randal! And how would *you* know anything about it, you—"

She was going to say "you mangy old sewer rat who works with his paws," but the sight of the flowers on the gold ring, and the suns and moons on the silver one, made her hold her tongue. She blushed in her ears, realizing that she must look rather mangy herself, with her dingy ribbon and ratted fur.

"But just think, you'd be famous," she said, changing tactics. "You and Montague have the same name. If the shells raised the money, your name would resound throughout the rat world!"

"Montague famous," Mr. Mad-Rat mused. He thought of the embittered young rat he'd met in the pipe after the Rat Chat—the young rat who'd cursed his name and who, he'd later realized, was the spitting image of "Mud-Rat," as he used to call his castle-crazy brother. He pictured the young rat brooding in a dark, dreary pipe somewhere downtown, little imagining that Montague was within screeching distance of the zoo at that very moment, scampering busily around the sunny park in search of money. Not five minutes ago, in fact, Montague had executed a daredevil maneuver outside the Monkey House just overhead, diving for a nickel under a vender's cart. "I suppose we could go today," Mr. Mad-Rat decided.

"Wouldn't if I was you, sir," Pembroke Pack-Rat advised promptly. "Can't trust people anymore'n mice."

"Oh, we can manage, can't we, Pem?"

"We!" The pack rat nearly dropped the shell painting he was holding in his paws. "I only deal with Pick-Person when he's alone."

"But of course you'll help!" Isabel said, fluttering her eyes a bit.

"Not me," the pack rat grumbled.

"Here I was thinking you were such a wonderful business rat," Isabel said, disappointed. "But I guess you only have a head for business on Mondays."

"What!" Pembroke croaked. "I got a head for business every day! Even at night!"

"But that's just what I thought!" Isabel began to repack the shells. "I'll come, too. It'll be fun—just like a field trip!"

"Fun, my eye," the pack rat snorted. "I ain't budgin'."

"Okay, then." Isabel held up the last shell. "What do you suppose they'll fetch, Mr. Mad-Rat? Dollars and dollars, wouldn't you say?"

"Wouldn't be surprised," Mr. Mad-Rat agreed with a smile.

"Well, let's go," said Isabel. "Good-bye, Mr. Pack-Rat. It was nice to meet you."

But Isabel and Mr. Mad-Rat had not gone far before the pack rat came sidling after them. And although Pembroke had not forgotten his marble sack, he mumbled that he might as well carry the matchbox, too.

At every turning in the new series of filthy gutters and drainage pipes, Mr. Mad-Rat stopped to catch his breath and pull the eyedropper from Pembroke's pack. They hadn't brought along the gold ring he'd decorated, but the swigs of wine got him singing a song about rings anyway.

> *Some rings hoop around the heart,*
> *From a lover, or a friend;*
> *But all are circles—none begin,*
> *And none will ever end.*

Finally, a slanting pipe, pitch-dark but for the yellow glow of the pack rat's eyes, led them up to a drain in what Mr. Mad-Rat explained was the basement of the towering temple of humankind housing Mr. Pick-Person's gallery. Stopping for wine seemed to be the only cure for Mr. Mad-Rat's shortness of breath, so it took them an hour to scale the flight of cliff-like stairs that led up out of the basement. At the summit stood a gigantic door, which was closed. Pembroke pushed his pack and the matchbox through the crack under it; then the three of them squeezed under, themselves. They were in a vast hallway with a waxed hardwood floor. Once Pembroke had loaded up again, they scampered across the hallway into a hole in the opposite baseboard.

There hadn't been a sign of a human being, but Isabel crowded near her peculiar new comrades as they passed down a dim, winding tunnel in the walls. It was curious how little she'd considered the field trip's real destination when she'd been coaxing them to come. She'd never been inside a den of humanity before; her fur was beginning to creep. But, fortunately, Mr. Mad-Rat, having caught his breath from the stairs, took up his ring song again, and this had a strangely calming effect on her.

Eventually, a pale glow suffused the tunnel. They came to the end, another arched opening, with a silver bell just inside it. Mr. Mad-Rat rang the bell very delicately, then unburdened Pembroke. In a moment, Isabel cowered back with a shriek. An enormous eye had appeared in the archway: a human eye.

"Is it Pick-Person?" Pembroke whispered.

"Hard to say on a Thursday, they all look so much alike," Mr. Mad-Rat replied. Once the eye moved back, he started pushing the matchbox out the hole, but Pembroke threw himself onto the box.

"Never show yer whole hand!" Pembroke urged in a hushed voice. "Not when you can play 'em one at a time."

The pack rat opened the matchbox and pulled out the top shell, the gardenia painting. As soon as he'd pushed it out, a pair of huge fingers—furless and fat and unwholesomely pink—plucked it away, sending a shiver down Isabel's spine to the tip of her tail. But the voice that spoke outside the hole was surprisingly soft and pleasant, for a human being's.

"Why, how lovely!" the voice said.

"Excuse me, sir?" said a harsher voice in the background.

"I just said, 'How lovely.' The song that bird's singing out the window."

"Is that the button, sir?" asked a third voice, thin and reedy.

"Button, Slim?"

Footsteps made the floor vibrate. "The brass one off my blazer. Didn't you just pick it up?"

"Uh, no, this is just—"

"A seashell!" Mr. Slim-Person exclaimed. "Hey, Mac, look what Mr. Pick's got!"

More footsteps. "This was on the floor?" said the harsh voice, apparently Mr. Mac-Person's. "Where'd it come from?"

"Look, a mouse hole!" Mr. Slim-Person pointed out.

"Mouse hole, indeed!" Pembroke muttered.

Again a horrifying human eye appeared briefly at the hole. "Good grief!" said Mr. Slim-Person. "There's a bell in there!"

"A *bell?*" Mr. Mac-Person said. "Hey, what's all this about, sir?"

Mr. Pick-Person just coughed.

"Get a load of the detail work on this shell!" Mr. Slim-Person exclaimed.

"Why, it's fantastic!" Mr. Mac-Person agreed. "Shouldn't we tear open the wall, sir, in case there's more of these things?"

"Certainly not," Mr. Pick-Person said.

"But, sir. We ought to find out where it came from."

Mr. Pick-Person heaved a sigh. "I have a pretty good idea already."

"You mean, you know who the artist is, sir?"

"Well . . ." Mr. Pick-Person took a deep breath. "I suppose it's the same artist who does our fancy ring work. I, uh, never mentioned this to anyone but my wife, because, well, because it's a *bit* hard to swallow

—but since you boys saw . . . You'll keep it strictly to yourselves?"

"Mum's the word, sir."

"Who's your man?"

Mr. Pick-Person coughed again. "Well, it's not exactly a man—a human man. That is, well . . . it's a rat."

Mr. Mac-Person laughed harshly. Mr. Slim-Person sucked in his breath in horror.

"It all started one day years ago when I found a gold band missing from the inventory," Mr. Pick-Person explained. "Must've dropped it on the floor or something."

Isabel, who had been rather curious about this herself, felt a nudge. "And Pem here found it," Mr. Mad-Rat told her. "Pem gets around, you know, and he knew I loved rings, so he showed it to me. First time I'd ever had gold to work with. Great stuff, gold—gets nice and soft."

"I didn't give the ring much more thought," Mr. Pick-Person was saying. "Then one day there it was, just this side of that little hole in the baseboard. Except, instead of a plain band, it had turned into the most beautiful ring you ever saw, all worked with lilies!"

"Nearly killed Pem when we gave it back," Mr. Mad-Rat confided to Isabel. "But once I'd done it up, I wanted some more raw material. Raw material's the thing, you know—it's . . . like having a horizon, as someone I know used to say. Anyhow, it worked out all right in the end, didn't it, old rat?"

"It's a living," Pembroke admitted.

"The next Monday, when the gallery was closed, I came in to try an experiment," Mr. Pick-Person was telling his employees. "I shoved another plain gold band into the hole, along with a bag of coins in payment for the work—and lo and behold, we've been doing business on Mondays ever since. But can you imagine the newspapers getting hold of it? 'Art Dealer Claims Rat Etches Rings!' Fact remains, though—his rings are the top of our line."

It took some time for his two employees to come to grips with this story. One after the other, they peered into the hole, nearly giving Isabel heart failure. But neither of these younger men could supply a better explanation.

"And this shell—it's *really* something," Mr. Slim-Person finally confessed. "Mrs. Plumpingham would give us thousands for it. Not to speak of the art museums."

"I guess he turned his paw to painting," Mr. Pick-Person mused. "It's his finest work yet."

"My finest work yet," Mr. Mad-Rat said with a pleased chuckle.

"Too bad we don't have any blank seashells around to give him in return," Mr. Pick-Person mused on. "I guess it'll have to be just money."

To Isabel's amazement, a twenty-dollar bill slid in

through the hole. She'd seen a few one-dollar bills in her time, and once a five, but never a twenty. Mr. Mad-Rat, however, shoved it right back out.

"Good grief!" Mr. Slim-Person cried. "It's no go!"

Soon a hundred-dollar bill came in. Mr. Mad-Rat crumpled it into a ball and kicked it out again.

"Excuse me a minute, gentlemen," Mr. Pick-Person said. "I have to go upstairs to the safe."

A door opened and closed out in the office.

"How much do you need for saving your wharves and making Montague famous, Miss Mumbly-Rat?" Mr. Mad-Rat asked, prying into Pembroke's marble sack.

"My father was aiming at another fifty thousand dollars," Isabel whispered, too grateful to resent his mispronunciation anymore.

"And how many shells are there in all, Pem?" Mr. Mad-Rat asked, pulling four eyedrop bottles from the pack.

"Ten, yer honor."

"Ten, eh. That would be . . . rmmmm, rmmmm—"

"Five thousand apiece, sir," Pembroke computed.

Mr. Mad-Rat drank different amounts of wine from three of the four eyedrop bottles so that each ended up at a different level. "Five thousand, eh," he said between sips. "Not a very round figure." Sip. "I prefer round figures." Sip. "Round things are best." Taking a coin from the bottom of Pembroke's pack, he began to tap the bottles. They produced one of the loveliest tunes Isabel had ever heard, a tune so enchanting that she felt sorry for the two human beings outside the hole, who were chattering on about money and their boss's "softness" instead of listening to the music.

The office door opened and closed again.

"My old emergency fund," Mr. Pick-Person announced.

"Thousand-dollar bills!" Mr. Slim-Person gave a thin, reedy whistle. "I've never seen one before!"

"A thousand dollars, sir?" Mr. Mac-Person complained. "To a *rat*?"

Sure enough, a thousand-dollar bill slid through the hole. Mr. Mad-Rat set down the coin, slid the bill back out, then resumed tinkling out his tune on the bottles.

"Good grief!" Mr. Slim-Person exclaimed.

The next offering was five of the thousand-dollar bills, the sight of which seemed to ignite Pembroke's yellow eyes so that they looked like two fireflies. "That'll do it," he croaked, rubbing his forepaws together. "Ten five-thousands make fifty thousand."

"Five thousand, fifty thousand," Mr. Mad-Rat mumbled, weighing the figures in his mind. "Not very round."

"But yer hon—"

Too late! Before Pembroke could stop him, Mr. Mad-Rat had dropped his coin and shoved the five one-thousand-dollar bills back out the hole.

"But Mr. Mad-Rat!" Isabel protested.

"Oh, call me Uncle Moony," Mr. Mad-Rat suggested, taking up the tune where he'd left off.

"Three months' wages!" Mr. Mac-Person sputtered, out in the office. "And the rat just throws it back in our faces! Why give him a red cent, sir? You've got the shell."

"Ah, but we do business," Mr. Pick-Person replied. "And besides, he may have more where this came from. I ask you—does this look like the work of a beginner?"

"No, sir, but . . . Not *more*! Why, that's—"

"I know how much it is, Mac. But don't forget, I've made a fortune off the rings over the years. And anyway, Mrs. Plumpingham will give me double what I'm shelling out—if you'll excuse the pun."

The sight of a wad of thousand-dollar bills coming

in the hole made Isabel feel faint. Uncle Moony set the coin aside to count them.

"Three . . . six . . . nine thousands, and two five-hundreds," he said uncertainly. "That doesn't sound so round either."

"But that's ten thousand, sir!" Pembroke yelped, flinging himself on the bills.

"Oh, ten thousand." Uncle Moony gave an approving nod and started to play once more. "Give him the rest, Pem—and so forth."

But Pembroke wasn't about to offer up the other nine shells all at once. He doled them out one at a time, each time collecting another ten thousand dollars. Except for a delay when Mr. Pick-Person sent one of his subordinates out to the bank, everything went smoothly. The last shell Pembroke pushed out was the one portraying a human child flying a kite.

"Mac! Slim!" Mr. Pick-Person exclaimed, after making the tenth payment. "Take a look at this one!"

Mr. Slim-Person whistled again. "Well, I'll be dog-goned," he said. "Or maybe I should say *rat*goned. Not only fine workmanship, but good taste in subject matter! True art! Unbelievable!"

"Mmm, it really is," Mr. Pick-Person said thoughtfully. "But then again, it's struck me before that Art and Rat are made up of the same letters."

Uncle Moony chuckled. Pembroke began counting the bills for the third time.

"Want me to pack up this here folding money, yer

honor?" the pack rat asked in a hoarse whisper when he'd finished the last recount.

"Why not, Pem?" Uncle Moony finished his tune on the highest-pitched bottle and tossed the coin aside. "I hope that'll keep Montague from cursing his name and help your wharves out, too, Miss Rumbly-Rat."

Isabel nodded numbly, watching Pembroke slip the discarded coin slyly back into his pack and stuff the bills in after it.

"Seems to be it for today" came Mr. Pick-Person's voice from out in the office. "I'll go up and stick our new acquisitions in the safe."

The office door opened and closed once more.

"No room for bottles," Uncle Moony remarked, seeing how plumply the bills filled the pack. "A shame to let good wine go to waste."

He pulled out one of the droppers and squeezed it into his mouth.

"A hundred thousand bucks!" Mr. Mac-Person muttered angrily outside the hole. "Can you believe it, Slim?"

"Five years' salary, to a rat!" Mr. Slim-Person agreed. "Tax free!"

"You wait here, Slim. I'll find out where this hole comes out."

"*I* know, Mac. The exterminator left a couple of those fumigating bombs in the basement. If we get the money, we split it, right?"

"Even Steven!"

"Great. But hurry—in case Pick decides to come back downstairs."

"What's a fumigating bomb, Uncle Moony?" Isabel asked, not at all liking the sound of the human conversation.

"Search me," Uncle Moony said, inserting the dropper back in the bottle. "But maybe we better be trotting along, and so forth." To Isabel's surprise, he took up the pack and fastened it onto her back. "There now, Miss Rubbery-Rat, that's not too heavy, is it?"

"Let me carry it, yer honor," Pembroke promptly volunteered. "It wouldn't be right, letting a wharf rat do all the work—especially such a one as you, miss."

Uncle Moony shrugged, so Pembroke transferred the plump pack to his own back. Casting a lingering look at his dandelion wine, Uncle Moony set off down the tunnel. Isabel followed, and the pack rat pulled up the rear with the precious cargo. When they came to the other end of the tunnel, Uncle Moony poked his head out. He yanked it back in just as a broom came down with a terrifying swish.

"Better backtrack," he advised. "Have to wait 'em out."

He herded them back to the eyedrop bottles and the empty matchbox at the office end of the tunnel. There he unburdened Pembroke, leaned back on the pack, and sampled some more wine.

"Comfortable, this paper money," he remarked. "Have a nip of wine, why don't you, Miss Bubbly-

Rat? You look like you could use a bit of fortifying."

This was a vast understatement. Isabel was trembling from the tip of her tail to the tip of her snout, and her paws were oily as could be. How in the world, she wondered, could this mangy wharf rat lounge there with his wine when he'd just missed by a whisker being flattened by a broom?

"Gad!" she finally managed to say in a quavery voice. "Are you sure they'll go away, Uncle Moony? I mean, we're *stuck* in here."

"Pick-Person's bound to come back down after a while, and even if he doesn't, they're big sleepers, these human creatures. They sleep for hours and hours in a row every night, like rocks, don't they, Pem? Besides, this isn't such a bad spot, is it? At least there's no wind, no rain, and so on." With this philosophical observation, Uncle Moony half closed his eyes and began to sing again.

> *This place or that, it's nearly the same—*
> *Stock-still, or out on a creep.*
> *In the long run you're stuck with yourself*
> *anyhow,*
> *In a hole or high on a heap—*

Suddenly the tunnel went black. A foul smell crept into Isabel's nostrils. Pembroke gagged.

"Uh-oh," Uncle Moony said. "Maybe *that's* a fumigating bomb."

Whatever was plugging the hole, it was certainly giving off a terrifying odor. Isabel heard Pembroke scamper off with a shriek—but she was too petrified with horror to budge. Holding her breath and trembling, she felt Uncle Moony fastening the pack onto her back again, then felt his tail loop around her neck like a collar. He pulled her down the tunnel.

It grew light toward the other end. Pembroke was cowering just inside the arched opening, croaking: "Gas—or the broom? Gas—or the broom?"

There was little time for choosing. A green cloud had followed them down the tunnel. But even in her panic Isabel wondered why Uncle Moony—who seemed so alert and sober now, not the least bit out of breath—why he had bothered to bring along the empty matchbox on his back.

"Count to five after I leave!" he commanded. "Then head for the door yonder as fast as your four legs can carry you! You both understand?"

Both she and Pembroke nodded. Then Montague Mad-Rat the Elder gave them a wink and darted out the hole with the empty matchbox on his back. Even as the broom came crashing down, Isabel obediently began to count.

"Missed him!" Pembroke croaked. "There he goes, miss! They're after him!"

". . . four, five!" Isabel cried, as the green gas crept into her nostrils.

She and Pembroke squeezed out the hole together,

which slowed them down a bit—yet, to her amazement, they weren't instantly flattened by a broom. The waxed hardwood floor was slick, and with the pack on her back she wasn't very quick on her feet, but Pembroke certainly didn't wait to help her under the door across the way. He dove under it and disappeared before she was halfway there. And when she reached it, the pack kept her from fitting through the crack. She had to roll onto her side and wriggle under.

The other side of the door was dim after the bright hallway, and she didn't think of the steep staircase down to the basement until she was tumbling over the first cliff-like step. Ouch! She let out a screech as she tumbled down a second step—and then a third—and then, just as she caught a topsy-turvy glimpse of Pembroke deserting her, squeezing through the drain at the foot of the steps, she fell off the side of the staircase—"Save meeeeee!" she cried—and plummeted into a horrible pit of darkness.

While Isabel was tumbling into the mysterious pit of darkness, Montague was lugging two pennies, one old and dingy, one shiny and new, to his laurel bush on the edge of the reservoir in the park. The afternoon was wearing on, and Montague was wearing out, not having taken a single breather from his treasure hunt. Three times, he'd risked life and tail. Three times, he'd barely missed being crushed—once by a saddle shoe, twice by loafers—while lunging for dropped coins. But still the pile under the bush was very disappointing to him. He'd had a stroke of luck near the carousel, it was true. But next to the quarter he'd found there, the best coin in his pile was a nickel, and of these he had only two. The rest were just pennies, and there weren't many of those.

After adding the last two pennies, he headed back out again, determined to do better. But by the time the sunset turned the reservoir the blushing pink of newborn ratlings, he'd managed to add only five more pennies to his store. He crouched there under the bush in the dying light and counted his collection. A paltry forty-seven cents in all.

Too depressed and weary to enjoy the colors the sky was turning, Montague sank down beside the coins and fell fast asleep. He dreamed that he was at the Grand Rat Chat. Up on the bench, Mr. Hugh Moberly-Rat was asking for contributions to R.R.R.—appealing for donations to save their way of life. He, Montague, dragged up to the bench a long sock filled with quarters and half dollars. As he tugged the sock full of coins across the bench to the dented beer can and donated it to the great cause, the thousands of rats assembled down below burst into applause so loud that he had to cover his ears. But he didn't cover his eyes, so he could see perfectly well how a beautiful young she-rat with a blue neck ribbon was deserting her reserved, front-row place beside young Randal Reese-Rat. Nothing young Randal could say could keep her there! She climbed up onto the bench and danced breezily across to the podium and gave him, Montague, a kiss on the snout . . .

Opening his eyes, Montague saw a full moon glimmering through the dewy branches of the laurel bush. He blinked uncertainly, still half asleep. His eyes were very sharp up to a certain distance, but the moon was awfully far away, and the shadowy splotch on its face was always a blur to him. More than once, he'd thought of painting the moon—gooseberry yellow on a blackberry background—but the blurriness had kept him from doing so. He blinked again. Was it blurry vision, or was there a circle around the moon tonight, a sort of halo? The words of a song drifted into his mind.

> *Rings are round the sun and moon,*
> *And inside of trees;*
> *Some are made by angel rats . . .*

Where had he picked that up, he wondered drowsily, still basking in the golden glow of the dream. Suddenly it all came back to him: running into his mangy, drunken uncle in the drainpipe; the shame of his name and the impossibility of the dreamed-of kiss. He squeezed his eyes shut on the moon.

Mercifully, he slept again. This time he tumbled into the sort of heavy, dreamless slumber that comes to rats only in the dead of winter or the depths of depression. When he next awoke, the sun was high in the sky, and little coins of sunlight were scattered among the real coins on the ground.

But the cheerful summer day didn't chase away Montague's new feeling of loneliness. What should he do with himself? Go home so his parents wouldn't worry, or take his forty-seven cents to Mr. Moberly-Rat? But his parents were always too busy working with their paws to worry about him, and as for the forty-seven cents, it hardly seemed enough to pester the great rat with. An oak leaf blew gently up against Montague's side. His tail flicked it away in disgust. It was a sign: he mustn't bother Isabel's father. For an oak leaf had served as the subject for one of the worthless shell paintings with which he'd humiliated himself in front of that noble rat.

The best plan seemed to be to hunt for more money. If he could gather a whole dollar, fifty-three more cents, perhaps that would be worth Mr. Moberly-Rat's time. But just as Montague was creeping out from under the bush, he overheard a conversation up above him.

"Now, that's what I caw-caw-call money," someone remarked. "Wouldn't you?"

"Of caw-caw-course I would," a second voice replied.

A pair of crows were bouncing down through the branches of the bush to investigate his pile of coins! Montague raced back and snarled as viciously as he could. The greedy black birds, who were bigger than he was, only snickered. He crouched there by his pile, waving his tail impatiently. Fifty-three cents would require every moment of daylight that remained. Fortunately, the birds finally got bored and flew away. But as Montague began to dig a hole to bury his money, he heard another voice nearby, grumbling.

"Idiot, idiot, idiot. Stupid, stupid, stupid."

Looking up from his hole, Montague watched a rat with a worn paper bag draped over his back come sidling in under the bush. The rat stopped and stared with deep interest at the pile of coins.

"Yours?" the rat asked.

Montague was dismayed to realize that the intruder was a pack rat, the very one he'd seen poking around the park before, the same seedy, yellow-eyed character who'd been with his uncle at the Grand Rat Chat. He was the last rat on earth Montague wanted to talk to, but the pack rat sank down with a sigh and, keeping his eyes fixed on the coins, began to complain about his lot in life.

"I used to have a real pack, you know, but now all I've got's this old bag," he grumbled. "Used to have a comrade—a wharf rat just like yer honor—now all I've got's myself. Used to have a lot of stuff, coins and everything, now all I've got's a headache from that green gas. I barely escaped with my life—heroic getaway, six brooms after me at once! And what do I get for it? Not a blessed thing! The miserablest, most unlucky rat in the city, that's who you're looking at, young sir."

"I doubt that," Montague muttered.

He bid the rat good day, but unfortunately the pack rat didn't take the hint to leave. For the sake of conversation, Montague asked him what had become of his comrade.

"Dead, more'n likely," the pack rat replied. "And

you know why? To raise money for a cause he didn't care about, and to keep some stupid nephew he hardly knew from cursing his name!"

To keep a nephew from cursing his name? "Dead?" Montague said, blinking.

"More'n likely. And to think how I ran off without my pack! And stuffed with all that wonderful folding money! It's enough to drive a rat crazy!"

"Dead?" Montague backed out of his half-dug hole. "You mean dead drunk, don't you?"

"I mean dead *dead*," the pack rat said testily. "And all to sell a bunch of stupid seashells and hand the lovely folding money over to a pretty little she-rat with beady eyes. *And* my pack!"

"Seashells?"

"With pictures on 'em. Fetched a tidy sum, too—tidiest sum *I'll* ever see. Oh, how could I be such an idiot!"

"What pretty little she-rat?" Montague asked, growing more alert by the moment.

"Some Mupperly-Rat or other, out for a cause."

"Moberly-Rat? Not Isabel Moberly-Rat!"

"Sounds warm. Came along on the expedition, and ended up with *my* pack! Just wrapped us around her tail like a ring, *she* did."

For a moment, Montague felt a spark of pleasure, realizing that Isabel must have thought better of his shell paintings than her father had. But then, no doubt, her only real interest in them was as a means of saving her wharves.

"You said something about keeping a nephew from cursing his name?" he pursued.

"*That's* how come he took the risk," grumbled the pack rat. "*He* didn't care two bits about money, never did, just that wife that up and left him, and doing up his rings—that's all *he* cared about. Usually, see, we just went Mondays. Mondays was safe."

Montague gulped. "But what makes you think he's dead?"

" 'Cause they were all after him. I mean, not *all*—the ones that wasn't after me. They must've figured he had the folding money in the matchbox. Yes, sir. That's how he figured they'd figure it, I figure."

"*Matchbox?* But where *was* all this? Shouldn't we go look for him?"

"*We?*" The pack rat sneered. "What do *you* have to do with the price of fish?"

"I'm Montague Mad-Rat, too," Montague declared.

"*What?* You're the *nephew?*"

Montague nodded. The pack rat blinked his yellow eyes, wonderingly at first, then thoughtfully.

"Well, maybe you're right, maybe we better go back," the pack rat finally concluded. "Old Pick-Person may have come to the rescue, after all. But we'll have to wait till midnight. The gallery's too unhealthy with all them Slim-Persons and Mac-Persons around. Mean as mud, they are—and greedy as devils. It'd turn yer stomach to see anybody as greedy as them."

"Midnight?" Montague said in amazement. "Your friend's in trouble and you want to wait till midnight?"

"I ain't budging till the moon comes up and the lights go out in all them buildings yonder," the pack rat stated. "There ain't nothing in the world could make me face them nasty, greedy creatures again *this* year."

Montague glared into the yellow eyes. But after a

minute his look softened. "How about forty-seven cents?" he suggested.

The yellow eyes widened, seeming to count the coins in the pile.

"Well, for forty-seven cents, maybe," the pack rat conceded. "You just turn yer back for a few minutes, young sir, and I'll bury them forty-seven cents somewheres nearby. I used to be a trusting soul, I did, soft as cottage cheese—but I learned *my* lesson. Gases and brooms! Everybody's so mean and greedy out there, it's enough to make you spit."

"Mmm," Montague said agreeably, turning his back to let the pack rat carry off his money and bury it nearby. For, oddly enough, it suddenly seemed more important to try to save his mangy uncle than the fancy wharves.

At this same noontime hour, Isabel was regaining consciousness—but instead of coins of sunlight scattered around her, her beady eyes blinked open on a dreary darkness. For the first instant, she assumed that she was at home in bed, waking up in the middle of the night from having eaten too much supper. And yet her bed felt awfully lumpy. And furthermore, it was ominously silent here. Where was the comforting whisper of the water creeping under the wharf? She took a deep sniff. Ick! Since when did her bedroom *stink*?

The smell was so horrid that she clapped her paws to her snout. Her paws stank, too! Staring up, she saw a pale, round opening high overhead. Everything came back to her in a rush. After escaping the green gas, she had squeezed under the door to the basement and tumbled off the side of the staircase into this pit of darkness. How long she'd been lying here dead to the world she couldn't imagine. All she knew was that the only thing that had kept her from being killed outright was the plump pack on her back, which had cushioned the fall.

Feeling the pack reminded her of its extraordinary contents. She jumped up. She had to get the money to her father to stop the poisoning of the wharves! But how slick and tall the sides of this pit were! After several attempts at scaling them, she fell back defeated on the ground.

But when had ground ever reeked like this? She sniffed around gingerly. Yuck! Fishbones, coffee grounds, ashes, rotten eggs, melon rinds. Something tickled her snout. Bugs were crawling around! Oh, lord! All at once, it hit her. She was in a garbage can. She—Isabel Moberly-Rat—was lolling in garbage with a bunch of bugs! Oh, wouldn't somebody save her? Not long ago, she remembered, someone had thrown her his tail. But the memory of the crushing broom kept her from squealing for help.

If she just sat there doing nothing but holding her nose, she would finally rot into garbage herself. So Isabel set to work. She spent the next three hours digging in the smelly refuse, hissing at the insects to keep away from her. Heaping the garbage on one side of the can, she eventually built herself a stairway. But when she tried it, the topmost stairs crumbled, and she tumbled all the way back down to the smelly bottom of the can. "Why'd you use coffee grounds at the top, stupid?" she muttered impatiently, trying to wipe herself off. Yanking a fishbone out from under a pile of orange peels, she dragged the bone up the crumbly stairs and leaned it like a ladder at the top. It didn't quite reach the rim. She carried it back down and got another fishbone as an extension, tying the two together with her neck ribbon, which was shot anyway. This double ladder did reach the rim; but just as she started up it she remembered the money and had to go all the way back into the stinky depths to fetch the pack, which she'd taken off in order to work.

At last, however, Isabel made it to the rim of the garbage can. How much better the world smelled from up there! Fortunately, there were several smaller cans nearby with their tops on, so she didn't have to drop all the way to the concrete floor. Once she got down, she scurried across to the drain, shoved the pack through the grating, and squeezed herself into the slanting pipe.

After the garbage can, the filthy underground pipes seemed quite luxurious to her. When she'd crept along for about an hour, she poked her head up through a grating to check landmarks. It was a sunny afternoon in the city. But was it still Thursday, or Friday now, or perhaps even Saturday?

Eventually, the pipe came out by some subway tracks. After looking both ways, she scampered across.

A couple of mice were huddled up against a switch-box. Except for the dormouse, Isabel had never stooped to speaking to the lowly creatures, but she did so now without the slightest hesitation.

"Could you tell me what day of the week it is, please?" she asked politely.

"What's wrong, can't you rats see?" one of the mice squealed.

"See what?" Isabel said, taken aback.

"Up there." The other mouse pointed his pitifully small tail up at the subway platform, which was mobbed with perspiring human beings. "See. They've all got suitcases—going away for the weekend. That means it's Friday, naturally."

Uppity little beasts, Isabel thought. But she didn't stay around to give them a piece of her mind. Friday! She'd spent a whole night and all the next morning lying unconscious in a garbage can! And who could say—by now perhaps the wharves were all poisoned!

It was rush hour when she came up out of the gutter across the street from her home. Wharf 62 was still standing: it didn't seem to have been turned into a parking lot yet. But the truck with the skull and crossbones on the tank was still in sight, parked in front of Wharf 58.

When a break finally came in the traffic, she lugged the pack across the street and into the slit in Wharf 62. The dormouse let out a bloodcurdling screech.

"No bums!" he screamed in a choked voice. "No

pack rats after business hours! Out of my lobby this instant!"

Isabel giggled. To think of the mouse mistaking her for a bum or a pack rat! But as she headed for crate 11, she felt her tail being yanked from behind, and she stopped giggling. How dare the dormouse pull her tail! But she didn't have to flick it away from him. The fire in her eyes did the job. The dormouse dropped her tail, and even, for just a moment, his perfect posture.

Isabel slipped into crate 11 by the back crack. Her mother was sitting in the kitchen with Mrs. Reese-Rat.

"Is Randal all right?" Isabel cried.

Mrs. Moberly-Rat took one look at Isabel and fainted. Mrs. Reese-Rat wrinkled up her snout and stared. Isabel hurried past them to the guest room, where she'd last seen her beloved, and flung open the door.

"Randal!" she cried in delight, as he sat up in the bedroom slipper. "You're alive!"

"Certainly, I'm alive," Randal said haughtily. "What's it to you?"

Isabel laughed her bright laugh as she crossed to the slipper. "It's me, silly. I've had the most amazing adventure! But all the time I worried about you."

Randal shrank back. "What do you mean by sneaking into the Moberly-Rats'," he bawled, "a common street rat like you? Good grief, what a smell!"

"Oh, that's only my fur. Gad, Randal, wait'll you

hear what I have in this pack! They'll never poison any of us again!"

"Mother!" Randal screeched, fanning in front of his snout.

"What's the matter?" Isabel asked. "Don't you want to marry me anymore?"

"Marry you! Are you crazy? Do you think a Reese-Rat would marry something like you!"

This speech knocked Isabel back a step. How could he treat her like this—or any fellow rat, for that matter? She took another step toward him. He made a face. She turned away, deeply hurt, and left the room.

Once she'd gotten a grip on herself, she crept down the corky hall and peered in at her father in his study. His fur seemed to have turned whiter with worry just since yesterday. After her experience with Randal, she realized she had better speak her piece as quickly as possible, so she hurried in and heaved the pack onto his dictionary.

"Here's a hundred thousand dollars, Daddy," she blurted out. "Half of it's for the Rat Rent, and half of it belongs to Montague. After all, he painted them. So everything's going to be fine. I'm sure Mr. Pier-Person's nephew couldn't get this much just for parking lots, especially seeing as the wharves are so old they'd collapse if they put cars on them anyway."

"Painted what?" Mr. Moberly-Rat cried, tumbling backwards. "Who in the Sam Hill are you?"

"I'm Izzy—can't you tell?" She brushed some coffee grounds off her fur. "Keep the other money for Montague, okay? I've got to go."

"What are you talking about?" her father said, growing stern. "What's all this babbling? The Rat Rent isn't a party game to joke about. The raising of funds isn't—"

"But I'm not joking, Daddy!"

"Izzy? Is that really you? What is this?"

"It's money. Open it and see."

For lack of any more sensible course of action, Mr. Moberly-Rat obeyed. His eyes grew to the size of nickels as he pulled out thousand-dollar bill after thousand-dollar bill.

"We sold those shells you wanted to throw out," Isabel explained. "The ones Montague brought. He painted them with his very own paws!" She wanted to go around the dictionary and give her father a hug, but remembering her odor she merely blew him a kiss. "Bye, Daddy. I'll be back as soon as I can."

Turning her tail on the flabbergasted rat, she went back into the corridor. Her mother, recovered from her faint, had started siphoning water into the ham tin.

"That *is* you, Izzy, I know your voice," Mrs. Moberly-Rat said shakily. "I'm running you a bubble bath."

"Thank you, Mother darling," said Isabel, scurrying past the plump figure. "But I don't have time for a bath right now."

"At least stop and have a bite!" her mother wailed. "There's some fresh goat cheese in the kitchen."

"No time, Mother," Isabel called back from the front crack. "I have to find Montague Mad-Rat to tell him about his shells."

But Montague already knew about the sale of the shells. He'd been hearing all about this and many other things from Pembroke Pack-Rat on the way from the reservoir in the park to Mr. Pick-Person's gallery. It had been a very slow journey, indeed. Every time Pembroke saw something shiny, he had to stop and inspect it, whether it was a torn candy wrapper or a thumbtack that had been washed down into the gutter. He collected several things for the old paper bag he was using for a pack, including a safety pin, a rusty fingernail clipper, and a button from the Museum of Natural History with a dinosaur on it. When he wasn't poking his snout into something, he would take up his horror story about the green gas and machine guns and hand grenades that had been used against him by human beings—once the greedy, nasty creatures had tired of using brooms and clubs and horsewhips. By the time they finally came up the drain in the basement of the gallery, Montague was somewhat less eager to visit these people than he'd been in the sunny park.

But still, Montague hurried the pack rat up the steep stairs out of the basement. His uncle, after all, had risked his life to keep him, Montague, from cursing his name.

When they peered through the crack under the door, Pembroke whistled under his breath. "What'd I tell you!" he croaked. "Look at them weapons! Look at the strength of the greedy creatures!"

Two human workmen in dusty overalls were prying open the wall directly across the hallway with crowbars. It was truly a terrifying display. Montague had never seen such destructive powers. He crouched there with his snout poking out just far enough to see, his own nervousness increased by Pembroke's shiverings beside him. Soon three other human beings in business suits came walking down the hallway. Their shoes echoed so loudly on the wood floor that Montague only uncovered his ears when the three came to a halt by the workmen.

"That there's Pick-Person, but them other two's part of the mob of murderers," Pembroke explained in a hoarse whisper.

"I still can't believe all this happened," said the one pointed out as Pick-Person in a surprisingly pleasant voice. "It's criminal—a breach of faith."

"But how could we stand around with our hands in our pockets while a rat ran off with a hundred grand?" a harsher voice wanted to know. "I bet it'll be here in the wall, sir. It must be, since it wasn't in this darn matchbox."

"Uh-oh," Pembroke whispered. "They got the matchbox."

Sure enough, Montague recognized the matchbox that used to stand like a trunk at the foot of his bed, now being flipped like a coin by a human being.

"But I gave him the money in good faith," the softer human voice protested, losing some of its softness. "I can't understand why you two took it upon yourselves to murder him—unless, of course, you're tired of working for me."

"But Mr. Pick, sir, he was only a *rat!*" pleaded one.

"And besides, sir," pleaded the other, "who's to say we murdered him?"

"Chasing him into an air-conditioning duct and then turning it on full blast! He's dead all right—frozen stiff."

"Frozen stiff," Montague whispered, shuddering.

"As soon as we finish here, sir," the harsh voice said, "we'll send these men upstairs to pull open the duct—so we can give him a proper burial. Okay?"

"What's a duct?" Montague asked.

"Search me," said Pembroke.

"Which way's upstairs?"

"That way," Pembroke replied, pointing left. "But we better—"

Montague heard no more, however, for he darted out from under the door. Going left required dashing between two of the towering legs in suit trousers; but just then the workmen started hammering the wall again, so neither the owner of these legs, one of the pair busy pleading for their jobs, nor any of the others noticed Montague. At the end of the hall, Montague found himself at the foot of another cliff-like staircase. Unlike the basement stairs, these were carpeted, easy to sink claws into, and he scampered up in no time. He crouched at the top and peered down another hall. What *was* an air-conditioning duct, he wondered. He racked his brain so hard over this question that he didn't hear the muffled footsteps climbing the carpeted stairs at his back. Suddenly an excruciating pain shot through him. He'd accidentally left his tail sticking out, and a huge shoe had come down right on it. Had there been no carpeting, his fine tail would surely have been flattened forever. But somehow he swallowed his screech, and the human being proceeded down the hall without noticing.

The human being appeared to be the one Pembroke called Pick-Person. As Mr. Pick-Person turned in at a doorway, Montague heard a yapping sound he recognized from the park. He gave his tail a painful twitch to be sure it was still working, then raced down the hall to the edge of the doorway.

"Sorry to have kept you waiting, Mrs. Plumpingham," Mr. Pick-Person was saying inside an office. "I'm afraid we've had a bit of a disaster."

"A disaster!" cried a lady who was sitting on—and filling up—a red-velvet couch. "What sort of disaster?"

Mr. Pick-Person coughed. "Well, uh, something to do with the artist who did that pinkie ring of yours, ma'am. At any rate, I've had to fire a couple of my employees."

In his wanderings through the park, Montague had run across countless human beings, but none, as far as he could remember, had ever approached the size of Mrs. Plumpingham. Nor had he ever seen one who sparkled so much. There were so many glittering rings on her plump fingers, so many jingling bracelets on her pudgy wrists, so many glinting diamonds in her stickpin, earrings, and tiara, such a blinding mass of gold in her yoke of a necklace, that it made Montague squint to look at her.

"I have some extraordinary works of art to show

you this afternoon, Mrs. Plumpingham," Mr. Pick-Person went on, turning to a massive safe in the wall. "They're seashells, painted in the most exquisite style. A perfect complement to your cameo collection."

"Oh, my!" Mrs. Plumpingham said enthusiastically, nodding her head so that her necklace vanished in a fold of her double chin. "Could I have one made into a brooch?"

Montague was staggered to think that things he'd painted with his own paws should require such grand protection as that safe—and deeply flattered to hear his shells called "exquisite." But pleasant as it might have been to hear this Mrs. Plumpingham-Person gush over his work, there was no time for dallying. Mrs. Plumpingham occupied nearly the entire couch, but squeezed in at her side, wearing a rhinestone collar, was a Pekinese. Montague had seen these silly, vain-looking dogs being walked on leashes in the park, though this was the first time he'd ever spoken to one.

"Excuse me, but do you know what an air-conditioning duct is?" Montague asked in his softest screech. He knew that dogs have excellent hearing.

"Naturally," the dog replied, giggling. "We have central air-conditioning at home."

"What do they look like, these air-conditioning ducts?"

"I'll only tell you that, my dear rat, on one conditioning—tee-hee."

"One condition?" said Montague, who was in no mood for jokes.

"Yes—that you pull your snout back into the shadow of the door. If *she* catches sight of you, she'll jump right out of her skin, and guess who she'll come down on top of!"

This request seemed reasonable enough, and once Montague had pulled his snout back, the dog answered his question.

"Air-conditioning ducts are sort of holes in the wall, with grilles over them. But why do you want to know, my dear rat? Are you hot? You really ought to avoid running around in the summer heat. It's very hard on the arteries, you know, and it wreaks havoc with your fur, not to speak of . . ."

But by this time Montague, seeing no grilled holes in the walls of that room, had dashed away. There were no grilled holes farther down the hallway either, so he dashed back the way he'd come. At the head of the stairs, there was just such a thing as the Pekinese had described: a stylish, floral-patterned grille, perfect for an art gallery, with a rose-shaped hole just big enough to squeeze through. The base of the grille was about a foot off the floor, requiring a running start, but on his second try he made the rose hole and shimmied through. He landed on the bottom of a cold metal shaft. Not a foot away from him, a mangy rat was lying on his side.

"Oh, Uncle Moony, please don't be dead!" Montague cried, though he knew very well that rats don't generally sleep on their sides. "Please wake up!"

His uncle's eyes didn't open. The mangy fur was icy to the touch. Montague pulled the tail—which bore, he noticed, a silver ring like his Aunt Elizabeth's. When this produced no effect, Montague flung himself on the rat and hugged him with all four paws. He blew warm breath on his uncle's whitening snout. Again nothing—not so much as a twitch of a whisker. How terrible that he could share a name with his uncle but not his body heat! Suddenly he remembered something from Pembroke's horror story of their adventures yesterday. Squeezing out through the rose hole, Montague dropped to the floor and raced down the carpeted stairs. He crept stealthily along the edge of the downstairs hallway and peered under a door near where the men were working. In that dim room, another office, there was a likely-looking hole in the baseboard. He squeezed under the door and scurried to the hole. Just inside were four eyedrop bottles. He wrapped his aching tail around the fullest of the four and carried it back upstairs.

Once he'd shimmied into the duct again, Montague unscrewed the dropper and forced it between his uncle's lips. As he squirted in some dandelion wine, his uncle sputtered. His eyelids quivered. Montague refilled the dropper and squirted in another snoutful.

"Brr-r-r-r." Uncle Moony blinked. "Where've I been, the dark side of the moon?"

"Oh, Uncle Moony, thank goodness!" Montague gave him a hug. "Come on, let's get out of here before they come and rip off the grille. They might mean well, but they give me the creeps!"

His uncle tried to stand.

"Curious," he remarked as he fell back on his side. "My joints don't seem to work."

"They froze you," Montague explained. "We have to get you out in the sun."

"And gold shall fill the afternoon," his uncle murmured fuzzily. "Yet silver's sweeter, sings the moon."

Montague pushed his uncle to the grille. Slipping out the hole, he pulled his uncle after him. They fell in a heap on the carpet.

"Are you all right?" Montague asked.

"I suppose so," his uncle replied. "I can't feel anything. Numb."

Montague flattened himself out on the floor and instructed his uncle to grab the fur on his back. Uncle Moony made an awkward load, especially on the way down the staircase, but downstairs the workmen were too busy ripping the wall open to notice the piggyback rats. When they reached the basement door, Montague shoved his uncle under and wriggled in after him.

"Yer honor!" cried Pembroke, who was still trembling there under his paper bag. "Yer alive!"

To the pack rat's dismay, Montague emptied the treasures out of the paper bag, but when he pulled it

up around his uncle like a sleeping bag, for warmth, Pembroke accepted the loss with a sigh. He even helped maneuver the half-frozen rat down the dangerous, uncarpeted stairs. When they reached the basement, they carried Uncle Moony along a peculiar trail of coffee grounds to the safety of the drain.

The underground trip from the gallery back to Central Park took even longer than the trip over. Carrying a half-frozen rat through the gutters and drainpipes was hard work. Every few steps, Montague and Pembroke had to set their load down to catch their breath.

The bars of sunlight shining down through the occasional gratings overhead turned to bars of weird, bluish light from the streetlamps. Toward the middle of the night, as they were passing under one such grating, Pembroke suddenly dropped Uncle Moony's hindquarters with a shriek and fled. A paw with bared claws had taken a swipe at them from above. Up on the grate, Montague made out a scrawny tomcat.

"Give him to me-me-meow!" the cat whined, showing his teeth. "I'm hungry!"

"Me, me, me, that's all those cats ever think about,"

Montague muttered, realizing that he was rather hungry himself. "Come on back, Pem! He can't reach us."

"Oh, why don't you let him go?" Uncle Moony suggested. "And you, too. I'll be fine here. One place is about the same as another."

But Montague was growing fonder of his uncle all the time, and although he set him down and scampered off down the pipe, it was only to drag Pembroke back. Soon they carried Uncle Moony out from under the grating.

"You don't really think I'd ever leave you, do you, Uncle Moony?" Montague asked at their next rest stop.

Uncle Moony sighed. He'd begun to realize that he would never do up another ring, for even though the underground pipes were quite warm, his joints showed no signs of loosening up.

"The best work I've ever done. That's what Pick-Person said about your shells, Monty. He's not a bad sort, Pick, for a person. I hope someday you'll do business with him yourself. You could get from Mr. Pick-Person, and give to that young Mr. Pier-Person—for the good of ratkind. After I'm gone, maybe Pem here would—"

"After you're gone!" cried Montague. "But you're going to be fine—all you need's a little rest and sunshine! Don't lose hope, Uncle Moony. We'll have you in the park by sunrise."

"But your parents'll be worried sick about you. Why don't you leave me and Pem here and run home to let them know you're all right?"

Montague gave a sniff. "They don't really care a hang about me," he explained. "My father just makes castles, and my mother just makes hats. He never even says good morning to me—and the only reason she knows I exist is I get her supplies for her." He stroked Uncle Moony's mangy head. "From now on, *you're* going to be my family. Okay?"

"You're probably underestimating your parents, Monty, as young rats often do—and you're probably overestimating me," Uncle Moony said. "Look at these paws. Can't even do up a ring anymore."

"But you risked your life because of me! No one ever risked anything for me before."

"I don't know about that. There was a pretty little she-rat, a Rumbly-Rat or some such."

"Oh, that was just to save her wharf," Montague told him.

"Hmm, think so?"

"Of course. Ready, Pem?"

"I suppose," Pembroke said with a groan, picking up his end.

At dawn, they finally reached the laurel bush by the reservoir. Montague and Pembroke immediately collapsed among the leaves under the bush. While they took their much-needed rat naps, Uncle Moony stared out across the wrinkled water at the pale silver round of the full moon, still hanging in the southern sky. The water made him think of his beloved Elizabeth, no doubt floating off to some exotic island. The young she-rat who'd talked them into taking the shells to Pick-Person had reminded him of her a bit, too, or at least of how she'd looked in her youth. What was that youngster's name? Stumbly-Rat? Jumbly-Rat? Frustrating not to be able to remember. "I guess I'm really getting old," he said to himself. "Older and colder all the time. Older, colder. Hmmm, might be a song in that."

If only he'd spoken louder! For, as it happened, Isabel, who would gladly have refreshed his memory, was only twenty-five yards away at that very moment, poking under a bayberry bush just across the bridle path. But laurel bushes don't produce berries, and keeping in mind Montague's bulging cheeks on their first encounter, Isabel was sticking to berry bushes in her search for him. She'd been at it all night and had wandered into some parts of the park that had given her the shivers. She hadn't rested since the garbage can, and she was bleary-eyed now, on the brink of exhaustion.

A pity we never had any ratlings of our own, Uncle Moony thought, watching the moon fade before the brightening sun. But as the sunlight grew stronger, he turned his eyes toward the shadows and saw his sleeping nephew. At least he'd had this chance to get to

know his namesake. It wasn't exactly like doing up a ring, but it was very nice.

Toward noon, when the sun was hot, both Montague and Pembroke woke up. Pembroke grumbled, pulling a bit of leaf out of his ear. Montague asked his uncle how he was feeling.

"Although Liza always seemed to think I was crazy," Uncle Moony said, "I've always found one place very much like another. But I have to admit this is a lovely spot, very scenic, and so on."

"Can you move your legs at all?"

"Hmmm. Not yet. Hot, though."

"I know what you need—food!" Montague exclaimed, pulling the paper bag off his uncle. "I'll go find some! I'm kind of hungry myself."

"Food," Uncle Moony said indifferently. "Pem, old rat, do you suppose you could wander down to the dandelion patch?"

"No money, yer honor," Pembroke replied. "We're flat—busted. They don't give credit on wine."

"But you're forgetting the forty-seven cents!" Montague said brightly.

"Oh, yeah," Pembroke mumbled, making Montague wonder if perhaps the pack rat *hadn't* forgotten the buried money. "I guess I could use that."

"I'll get some food while you go for the wine," proposed Montague. "Uncle Moony, you just soak up the sun!"

Following Pembroke under the next bush, Montague watched him dig up the coins and toss them into his paper bag.

"I don't like it," the pack rat grumbled, slinging the bag over his shoulder. "He hasn't sung a single song. Not like him. Ope*ratic*, he is, singing all the time."

"Let's hurry!" Montague said. "I'll meet you back here in fifteen minutes. I *know* we can make him better!"

With that, Montague pattered across the footbridge over the bridle path and passed by the very bayberry bush where Isabel had been early that morning. From there, habit led him straight—or crookedly, actually—to the prime berry patches by the Great Lawn. Would his Uncle Moony even care for berries, he wondered. Montague wasn't wild for them himself —but he was awfully hungry. He gave a bush a shake. A nice, ripe blackberry fell at his hind feet. Just as he reached for it, a warbly voice spoke up behind him.

"Montague Mad-Rat, by any chance?"

He whirled around. There stood a she-pigeon, head twisted, one eye fixed on him.

"How'd you know my name?" Montague asked.

"Guessed. Heard you like berries. Wait here."

The pigeon gave a leap, spread her wings, and flew up between two berry bushes into the sky, leaving Montague thunderstruck. Only a few days ago, he'd hardly been acquainted with so much as a rat outside his immediate family—and now a strange pigeon knew his name! For a minute he didn't budge, mulling over the mystery of things. But soon he remembered his mission. No, he wouldn't touch a bite himself. First, he would collect berries for Uncle Moony. He felt quite lighthearted as he shook another bush. How lucky to be the namesake of such a wonderful rat! The manginess and the drunken songs only made him better. Ouch! But Montague didn't mind the thorns on the low-lying brambles as he raced from bush to bush. After filling his left cheek, he quickly started on the right, suddenly remembering that, so far, he'd forgotten to beg his uncle's forgiveness for the time in the drainpipe after the Grand Rat Chat. It hurt much more than the bramble thorns, that memory of turning his back on Uncle Moony. He couldn't wait to get back to apologize and give his uncle a hug.

As he squeezed in one last berry, he heard a new sound, a pattering in the underbrush. Three young wharf rats poked their heads out of the tall grass nearby.

"Mad-Rat?" they asked.

Oh, no, Montague thought, shaken by his old shyness. Young wharf rats out to make fun of his name and his berry-filled cheeks again. As half a dozen more of them popped out of the tall grass, Montague turned tail and scampered away.

His escape route led out onto the edge of the Great Lawn. Instead of ripping a wall apart with crowbars, the human beings here were taking turns smashing a ball with a bat. Montague headed toward the other end of the grassy field, which was mercifully empty, to circle back to the reservoir. Or was it empty? He must be dizzy from hunger, he decided, for swarms of black dots began to appear before his eyes. He blinked. But the dots refused to vanish. The dots started to look less and less like dots—more and more like rats. They *were* rats—rats swarming out over the Great Lawn in droves! What on earth were so many rats doing in the park, even on a Saturday? Montague looked over his shoulder. More rats—by the hundreds! And they all seemed to be coming at *him*! What on earth had he done? He shivered and gave a screech, turning the berries in his cheeks to pulp.

The swarms were closing in on him from north and south. Where could he escape? In an oak tree on the edge of the lawn he saw a squirrel hole, about as high up the trunk as the air-conditioning duct had been up the gallery wall. He made for it at top speed and just managed to scramble up the bark into the hole before the nightmare mob converged on him.

Luckily, the squirrels were out, perhaps gathering their nuts. He'd never cared for squirrels, with their showy tails, but at least they seemed to be neat creatures, with paper cups for wastebaskets. He spat the crushed berries into one.

His fur stood on end. Outside the hole, a chorus of bloodthirsty voices was rising up in a horrid chant.

"Come on!" shrieked the mob. "Tigoo that rat!"

What on earth was "tigoo," Montague wondered—though perhaps he was better off not knowing. Rats began to pour in through the hole. Montague backed up to the rear of the chamber. He was cornered . . . like a miserable mouse. He bared his teeth, thinking the berry juice might look like blood and frighten them. But on they came, closing in on him, so he just shut his eyes and prayed for it to be over quickly.

While the chanting mob was cornering Montague, Pembroke Pack-Rat was having problems of his own. Pembroke set off from the reservoir to fetch the dandelion wine at the same time Montague set off for the food, but Pembroke was in less of a hurry.

"Going to bed at dawn," he grumbled, hiking the paper bag with the forty-seven cents in it up on his back as he crossed the bridle path. "It's one thing for old Mad-Rat—we *carried* him all night. And it's one thing for that nephew—young rats can bounce back. But I'm not as young as I used to be."

The farther Pembroke got from the reservoir, the more sorely tempted he was to make a clean getaway. Why should he spend the only money he had in the world, his last forty-seven cents, to buy spirits for a mangy old rat whose joints were all frozen up? The long and the short of it was that old Mad-Rat would never be able to do him an ounce of good anymore. It was plain as the snout on his face: no more ring work, no more business. And what did he, a tried and true pack rat, care for anything but business? Here he'd just stayed up the whole night straining every muscle in his body carrying the old fellow through drainpipes, and what thanks did he get? He was asked —ordered, really—to give up his savings!

Instead of heading south, the direction of the dandelion patch where the wine came from, Pembroke turned north. After a few minutes, he slipped out at the top of the park. He hustled across the sidewalk and started slouching along underneath the cars parked by the curb. Sometimes, when human beings got out of their cars, money fell out of their pockets into the gutter. Once, in fact, he'd found a red-satin change purse containing three dimes, three nickels, six pennies, a skeleton key, and a mess of hairpins. He wished now he hadn't traded that purse to another pack rat for a rare Indian-head nickel. Red satin wasn't quite to his taste, but it would have been better than this crummy old paper bag. He shrugged the bag off, seeing something shiny beside a back tire. Just as he reached his prize, he felt an oozy sensation on his fur.

Pembroke twisted his head around to look. Oh, cripes! A big black drop of oil had dripped out of a crankcase and landed squarely on his back! Oil, of all the lousy liquids! You couldn't lick oil off of you, because it tasted so horrible, and you couldn't rub it off, because it got your paws all sticky. To make matters worse, the shiny thing turned out to be only a tab from a beer can! Pembroke rolled over on his back and squirmed, trying to rub the oil off that way. Even pack rats don't like to be dirty. But the pavement was hot and dusty, and squirming only made things messier.

He thought of the reservoir, of washing there. And all of a sudden he realized: the black oil drop from the crankcase was a judgment, a sign from above. For, truth be known, the forty-seven cents in the bag wasn't quite *all* the money he had in the world. Over the years, old Mad-Rat had given him a fair wage, besides which he'd skimmed off half of the coins Pick-Person had paid for the ring work, and these coins were buried in a hundred and fifty-four secret spots in Central Park.

The least he could do, Pembroke supposed, was fetch the poor old sot his wine. Hefting the bag onto his back again, he scooted back into the park. But soon his feet began to drag. In spite of the oily sign from above, parting with the forty-seven cents, now that he'd gotten used to the feel of it, seemed hard. He stopped by a horse-chestnut tree and looked about warily. Vicious rats sometimes hung around up in this neck of the park. But there was no one in sight, not even a grasshopper, so Pembroke dug down between two of the horse-chestnut tree's roots. He unearthed seventeen cents, which he'd buried here last fall. Adding three pennies from the bag made it an even twenty cents, a rounder sum, easier to remember. After reburying this and carefully raking the ground with his claws, he proceeded to a granite boulder not far off. He stepped off three body lengths due east from a cleft in the rock and dug up two tarnished quarters. It was all he could do to keep from adding the quarter in the bag to these, for the idea of three secret quarters lying side by side underground was almost irresistible. He contented himself, however, with adding a nickel.

Pembroke made several more such stops to boost his morale, and by the time he reached the dandelion patch near the foot of the park the forty-seven cents had dwindled to thirty-one: a quarter, a nickel, and a penny. It was an enterprising family of field mice who fermented the dandelions into wine. These industrious little creatures didn't care a straw about money; they did the work because they enjoyed it and because they liked to tipple a bit in the evenings. But, unfortunately, an unscrupulous agent—who happened to be one of Pembroke's second cousins—had them under his paw. He supplied the eyedrop bottles, which the mice rather liked, and he peddled their wine on the side. Crafty as this cousin was, however, Pembroke managed to convince him that he had only twenty-six cents in his bag, leaving himself a nickel.

oor Montague, however, didn't even have a penny. As he cowered in the squirrel hole on the edge of the Great Lawn, all he had to offer the bloodthirsty mob was his life. They closed in on him, and he covered his face with his paws.

But instead of tearing him instantly to pieces, the rats lifted him up and carried him to the mouth of the hole. So everyone would be able to see? Montague wondered, opening his eyes a fraction. In the far distance, human beings were running away as fast as their two legs could carry them. In the foreground, a vast gray sea of rats covered the entire bottom half of the Great Lawn, rats of every description, even more than had attended the Grand Rat Chat. At the sight of him, they let out what sounded almost like a tremendous cheer! Then the cheer turned into the chant again. From the mouth of the squirrel hole, Montague could hear it more clearly. It wasn't "Come on, tigoo that rat!" It was simply "Montague Mad-Rat!" they were shouting, over and over and over. Montague's eyes opened wider. The thousands of rats weren't going to tear him limb from limb at all, weren't even making fun of him. They were shrieking and waving in admiration, sending his name resounding to the skies!

But, although it was a relief to know that he wasn't about to die, Montague was too shy to take immediate pleasure in all this attention. He shook his head, to try to get them to stop chanting. This, however, only encouraged them. Taking it as an acknowledgment, the mob just chanted louder. Montague turned to the rat standing next to him. Putting his snout up to this rat's ear, he asked at the top of his lungs what on earth was going on. "How do you all know my name?" he cried.

"Everyone's been looking for you!" the other cried back in delight. "Pigeons helping—mice, too. All scrounging suspended till we found you. Hooray!"

"Hooray for Montague Mad-Rat, savior of ratkind!" the crowd responded.

"Savior of ratkind?" Montague echoed. "What do they mean?"

"The money from your shells!" the nearest rat yelled out. "Young Mr. Pier-Person found it in the barrel yesterday evening with the regular coins, and all the poisoning's stopped. We can keep our homes! Hooray!"

"Hooray for Montague!" echoed the crowd.

All the thousands of rats were waving their paws at him as if he were their oldest and dearest friend. Montague began to shed a bit of his shyness. It was just like his dream, only better! Lifting his right paw tentatively, he gave a friendly wave. The crowd roared. Montague flashed a smile. The crowd went wild, screeching and hopping up and down. He tried smiling and waving at the same time. The crowd went crazy. It was pandemonium.

The cheering might well have gone on all afternoon if a trio of well-fed, middle-aged rats hadn't made it their business to scramble up the trunk to join Montague on the lip of the squirrel hole. These were political rats, experts at handling crowds, and after many grand gestures they restored a measure of order. But, though each wanted to be seen right beside Montague, the lip of the hole was only wide enough to accommodate one rat on either side of him, so the fattest of the three was squeezed out and tumbled back into the crowd, headfirst.

"Montague the Magnificent!" bellowed the louder of the two remaining political rats.

This exclamation brought on more thunderous applause. Montague began to smile and wave again. Soon he discovered that by smiling directly at young she-rats near the trunk, he could make them faint.

During the next ovation, he caused over a dozen fainting fits.

As that ovation began to peter out, the crowd parted to make way for a rat carrying a foil packet. This new rat was helped up to the hole while the others moved respectfully back from the lip.

"My fellow rats!" screeched none other than Mr. Hugh Moberly-Rat, as he laid a paw on Montague's shoulder. "My dear companions in rathood! Through the help of my daughter, who unfortunately passed out from utter exhaustion this forenoon, after searching all night long for our friend here . . . I say, through information provided by my own sweet girl, who by ill luck is currently collapsed at home, we have located our young savior in the berry patches of this great, green park!" Noisy cheers. "What a thrill it is for me"—Mr. Moberly-Rat's piercing tones rose above the cheers—"what a privilege to have the honor of standing beside a true, a genuine artist! For it was through this young rat's works of art, paintings of so rare a quality, so entrancing a nature that no one could fail to be moved by them on first sight . . . through these indisputable masterpieces of his that this prime specimen of young rathood saved our wharves!" Standing ovation. "How can we honor such a savior?" Mr. Moberly-Rat screeched on, patting Montague's shoulder enthusiastically. "What homage can we pay to such authentic genius? Unfortunately, human beings consider this many rats in the park an unlawful gathering. For some reason, they frown on seeing us in such vast numbers. So might I suggest we adjourn downtown to Wharf 62, therein to heap Montague the Magnificent with our formal congratulations?"

"Hooray!" shouted the crowd. "Hooray for Montague the Magnificent!"

Wharf 62! Montague thought in delight. Perhaps Isabel would revive when they all got there and give him another kiss on the snout, as she had when they first met! In preparation, he ran a paw across his snout, wiping off the berry drool. Then he raised the paw in another wave, sending the crowd into ecstasies and further shouts of "Montague the Magnificent!"

When at last Pembroke Pack-Rat arrived at the laurel bush by the reservoir, he was rather surprised to see that he'd beaten the nephew back. Old Mad-Rat looked in a pretty sad way, but the wine revived him a bit. After giving him several squirts, Pembroke climbed down the stone bank to the reservoir to wash the oil off his back. This done, he shook himself dry, climbed the bank, and gave his old partner another squirt of the wine, inquiring politely if it was a good vintage.

"Tip-top, Pem," Uncle Moony replied, trying to sound cheerful. "Very kind of you to fetch it. Thought I might have seen the last of you."

"What!" Pembroke croaked in outrage. "You think I'd run out on you?"

"Well, I thought you might be getting tired of me.

After all, that sewer under the zoo's so steamy, and you've been stuck down there with my singing all these years, and so on and so forth."

"But I'm partial to yer singing, what with me and my croaky old pack-rat voice," Pembroke insisted. "How about giving us one now?"

"I'm sorry, Pem, but I'm afraid I'm not quite up to it. But . . ."

"What, yer honor?"

"Well, I hate to trouble you anymore, Pem, after all you've done these last couple of days. But I wonder if you could do me one more little favor."

"Just name it," Pembroke said, pleased to be appreciated for once.

"Go find my nephew, Monty. There's something I want to give him."

"But he'll be back in two shakes of a rat's tail. I'm surprised he ain't back yet. He just went to fetch you a nibble."

"I know, Pem, I know. But, to tell you the truth, I'm not really hungry, and I was thinking maybe you could hurry him along."

"Sure thing. Another squirt before I go?"

"Thanks, Pem, old rat."

The squirts of wine were very warming to the insides, and as Pembroke slouched away, Uncle Moony began to cherish a hope of seeing the moon rise once again over this lovely reservoir. Staring at the mysterious creep of the water, he'd started to understand the attraction sea travel had for his beloved Elizabeth. What a narrow life he'd always lived! And yet it was awfully hard to keep his eyes open, and each time his lids drooped shut, it wasn't the creeping water he saw in his imagination but rings—rings of sunny gold and moonlike silver worked with the designs of his own paws. In a way, it was good that he hadn't eaten in so long, for he could sense that his tail had lost a bit of weight, so that the ring there would be easy to work off. If only Montague would hurry! Br-r-r-r! The sun had traveled so far across the sky that a shadow of the bush was creeping over him now. Suddenly he was back in the air-conditioning duct, a blast of cold combing back his fur, the metal icier and icier under his paws . . .

"Yer honor? Wake up, yer honor!"

Was that a broomstick poking him? Forcing his heavy lids open, he saw two blurry yellow circles. No, it was Pembroke. He was in the park, waiting for Montague.

"Back already?" Uncle Moony murmured.

"I saw him, yer honor, but I couldn't get near him!" Pembroke croaked excitedly. "He's in a hole in this tree, and there's a million rats all around it, and he's waving at 'em, and they're all jumping and cheering like there's no tomorrow! I wish you could move yer joints, I'd take you over to see!"

"Like there's no tomorrow," Uncle Moony whispered. Well, he thought with a smile, that was a much finer present than the one he'd had in mind. "That's wonderful," he added weakly.

"Wonderful, yer honor? Why, I never seen anything like it in my born days! Did I say a million? More like two—two million rats, all screaming like they've gone crazy! You want me to try and carry you? It's not far, just over on that big lawn. Yer honor? Come on, yer honor, wake up."

Many paws helped Montague down from the squirrel hole, but he never touched the ground. He was carried off on the backs of other rats toward the foot of the park, at the head of a grand procession. At the sight of the procession, young human beings on roller skates and skateboards skidded to screeching halts, and human nursemaids with their baby carriages turned and raced off at full tilt. But Montague, riding aloft at the front of the parade, had never felt finer in his life. To think that his shell paintings, which he'd done just for fun, should lead to this! To think how he used to make this trip down the park, zigzagging through the shadows of the underbrush and the benches to keep from being seen! And now the entire rat world was fighting for glimpses of him —him, Montague the Magnificent!

Once he got used to the sensation of being carried, he leaned back on the paws supporting him, to appreciate the scenery. He looked straight up. Trees filtered the ripe, late-afternoon sunlight. But although the trees were still, a roar gathered at his back like a great rustling of leaves. "Hooray for Montague, the great shell painter!"

Montague twisted around to smile and wave in acknowledgment of the compliment. The procession was passing a pond off to the left, and even it was ripe and golden in the slanting light, as if sunshine were like rain and, after pouring down all day, could collect in a vast puddle.

". . . genius of his generation!"

After giving another modest wave, Montague looked lazily out ahead. How lovely! Even the grassy field was golden! But as the procession approached the field, Montague saw his mistake. It wasn't covered with golden grass at all but with little yellow flowers. Dandelions.

"Hooray for Montague, savior of ratkind!"

Suddenly it was as if all the paws underneath him had started to pinch. Dandelions . . . "savior of ratkind." Montague squirmed. Dandelion wine! His uncle! Of course! It was Uncle Moony, not he, who had saved the wharves! How could he have been so carried away as to forget? And what about the food he was supposed to fetch?

"Wait a minute, let me down!" he shouted, twisting around again. "There's been a mistake! I'm not the one you want. It's all a mistake!"

The procession ground to a halt. But the lead rats refused to set him down.

"You're Montague Mad-Rat, aren't you?" one of them called out.

"Yes, I am," Montague replied, "but—"

"And you painted the shells, didn't you?" asked another.

"Well, yes, I did, but—"

"No mistake about it!" they chimed. "You're the savior of our homes!"

"But I'm not the one who got the money!" Montague shrieked. "I'm only Montague Mad-Rat the Younger. It's my uncle who's the hero. Does anybody have any food?"

"I believe my wife packed me a little cheese," Mr. Moberly-Rat admitted, sniffing his foil packet. "Cheddar, I think—quite sharp. Are you hungry, Montague?"

Montague crouched and sprang from the bed of paws.

"Come with me, sir!" he yelled, landing out in front of the parade. "Please—and hurry!"

Off Montague raced, back up through the park, back up along the edge of the Great Lawn. As a rule, he went around the thickest brambles, but he was so upset with himself now that he hurtled right through them. As a rule, he used the footbridge over the bridle path around the reservoir, but now he threw caution to the wind, darting straight across the open cinder track. Yet none of the horses trotting down the path crushed him under their hooves. For the whole rat procession, not just Mr. Moberly-Rat, had followed Montague, and the horses, seeing not the usual two or three rats but thousands of them, reared up and galloped off with their riders in the opposite direction.

Montague dashed up the bank and stopped abruptly at the laurel bush, causing the rats just behind him to tumble over one another. These were all young rats. The older ones, like Mr. Moberly-Rat, were still huffing and puffing up the bank.

"There's your hero!" Montague declared, pointing under the bush.

A young rat who had bristly whiskers for his age went up and poked Uncle Moony.

"This mangy old thing?" The rat sniffed at an open eyedrop bottle nearby. "Why, he's soused as a mouse."

"He's not a mangy old thing!" Montague objected.

Several rats snickered. "*That's* the savior of rat-kind?" said one. "A likely tale!"

"He nearly froze to death saving your wharves," Montague retorted, rounding angrily on the speaker.

"Nearly?" said the one with the bristly whiskers. "But he's not soused, he's a goner."

"No, he's just sleeping from staying up all last

night," Montague explained, relieved to see the crowd parting to let Mr. Moberly-Rat through. "May I have that cheese, please, sir?"

Mr. Moberly-Rat, who was panting, handed over his foil packet. Montague unwrapped the piece of sharp cheddar and held it under his uncle's snout.

"Food, Uncle Moony!" he coaxed. "Wake up!"

Uncle Moony didn't stir. Startled to see that his uncle was now lying in the shade, Montague began to wonder just how long he'd stood smiling and waving from the squirrel hole.

"Pem! Come help me move Uncle Moony back in the sun!"

The dandelion wine told him that Pembroke must be around, but his call received no answer.

"Is there a doctor out there anywhere?" shrieked Mr. Moberly-Rat, who had now caught his breath.

As a general ratitioner squeezed out of the crowd of onlookers, Montague grabbed the eyedropper and squirted some of the golden wine between his uncle's lips. It dribbled out. Uncle Moony's eyelids didn't flutter.

"Come along, son," the general ratitioner advised, trying to lead Montague away. "That's not going to help."

Mr. Moberly-Rat came up to examine Uncle Moony, too. The great rat leaned close, to listen for breathing. "Goodness!" he exclaimed, startled. "I think he whispered something!"

"Whispered?" Montague cried, jerking away from the doctor. "What?"

"Well, it sounded like 'Wonderful.'"

The general ratitioner put his ear up to Uncle Moony's chest.

"Doubt that," he declared. "He's dead."

"But I could have sworn he whispered," said Mr. Moberly-Rat.

"It was probably the wind," the doctor diagnosed. Indeed, a breeze had sprung up, sweeping across the reservoir and rustling the dry leaves of the laurel. It made Montague shiver.

"You must be right, nobody dies saying 'Wonderful,'" Mr. Moberly-Rat conceded. "Come along now, Montague. Your uncle will be given a hero's burial. Right here under the laurel is fitting—most suitable."

As other rats tried to usher Montague away, he grabbed desperately onto his uncle's tail. The others' lips were moving, but the breeze in the leaves and a queer pulsing in his ears kept him from hearing. Oh, but it was all right—the tail was stony cold, but there was no ring on it! This was a different old rat!

Or was there a worn band around the base of the tail from which a ring might have slipped on the way from the gallery?

Holding his breath, Montague stared hard at the side of the face. It was his uncle's—the face he'd turned from in disgust in the drainpipe. Gradually, the breeze died, and the leaves all quieted down like an audience expecting a song.

"Hey, you're not going to start crying on us, are you?" asked the young rat with the bristly whiskers.

Montague stared around at the unfamiliar gray faces closed in around him. These strangers began prying his uncle's tail out of his paws. And why were those others digging a hole in the ground?

"Come along now, you of all rats ought to set a brave example," an elderly rat advised. "After all, you're Montague the Magnificent."

With all his might, Montague tried to crawl back to bury his wet face in his uncle's mangy fur, but paws were tugging him away toward the bank. He craned his head, searching desperately for the pack rat. "Pem, tell them, *he's* Montague the Magnificent!" he tried to shout. But as he was dragged into view of the rat multitude crowded below, they let out a great cheer, and his voice wasn't strong enough to be heard over it. In fact, his words caught in his throat, or perhaps in his heart, and all that came out was a little sob—more like a ratling than a hero.

Pembroke, meanwhile, was over a mile away, in the rose garden by the Central Park Zoo. The beetles nibbling the rose petals up above saw only a crumpled paper bag bumping along the ground, but Pembroke was under it. The bag contained a nickel, the one he'd managed to keep from his crafty second cousin at the dandelion patch. It was this nickel that had released him from the bush by the reservoir. After trying in vain to wake old Mad-Rat up, Pembroke had held the nickel under his former business partner's whitening snout and hadn't detected any breath misting the coin.

"Funny there's no money by this sidewalk," Pembroke said to himself as he crept along, peering left and right from under his bag. "Some other rat must've covered this territory lately, devil take him. Just my luck. Like the old coot croaking on me, just when I was starting to build up a bit of a nest egg . . . Hmmm, there's twenty-two cents behind that white rock over there . . . Leaving me in the lurch like this. 'Like there's no tomorrow . . . That's wonderful!' Some last word—wonderful! Not for me, it ain't. But then, who ever gave *me* a thought? All *he* cared about was them rings and singing mushy songs about love. Hmmm, thirty-five under that birdbath, plus the nickel, that would be an even forty . . . hmmm. . . . Listen to me, he's gone half an hour and I'm already babbling to myself for company! Well, it was a pretty good thing while it lasted. But actually I didn't get that much out of it, not half what I deserved, doing all his business for him all these years . . . Oh, cripes!"

A rose thorn had snagged his paper bag, leaving Pembroke temporarily exposed. At the same moment a plump ladybug, who was enjoying a break from her luncheon on a rose leaf up above, happened to glance down. And the ladybug stared—for it wasn't an everyday sight, a coarse old pack rat with shifty yellow eyes, wearing such a lovely, delicate silver ring on his tail.

The sewer was smoky as ever. Fires were smoldering under the soup cans, and Mrs. Mad-Rat was dipping feathers into the dyes. The younger rats were quarreling; the ratlings were whimpering. Up on the slope, Mr. Mad-Rat was putting the finishing touches on his hundred and seventh mud castle, while scouting, out of the corner of his eye, possible sites for his hundred and eighth.

At the sight of Montague, Mrs. Mad-Rat dropped a bright purple feather in the dirt.

"Monty! Are you all right? I've been worried sick! Two dinners in a row you've skipped!"

Not worried enough to stop dyeing her feathers, Montague thought, creeping into his bed.

His mother came over to his bedside. "Don't you want a nibble, dear?" she asked.

Montague shook his head.

"Where've you been?"

"The park, mostly."

Mrs. Mad-Rat glanced around a little uneasily. "No supplies, I see. I'm nearly out. Want to see the hats I've done?"

A tear trickled down Montague's snout. "I don't think I'll be collecting any more supplies, Mother. I don't think I'll be doing anything."

His mother wiped a paw on her fur and began to stroke him tenderly. "Why, Monty, whatever's the matter?"

"Uncle Moony's dead," he moaned. "Thanks to me."

"Moony dead!"

"And I left him alone to die. I was bowing and waving to the crowd instead of keeping him in the sun."

"Bowing and waving to the crowd?" His mother felt his ears and the tip of his snout. "No temperature," she decided. "You haven't been nipping dandelion wine, have you?"

He shook his head.

"Moony dead!" she repeated. "Preserve us! I think Liza's ship's due in this coming Tuesday. Poor dear, she'll be shattered."

"A lot she cared about him," he said with a snort.

"Of course she cared, dear. It's just her nature got in the way. They weren't as well suited as your father and I."

Montague cast a skeptical glance up the muddy slope. A ratling let out a screech. Montague pulled the covers over his head.

"What crowd was this you were bowing to, dear?" his mother asked, pulling the covers back down.

Only a few minutes ago, Montague had been surrounded by thousands of rats, escorting him out of the park. But their admiration had been unbearable, and knowing the gutters as he did, he'd managed to dive into one and give them the slip. "Oh, nothing," he

muttered. "They got me mixed up with someone else, that's all."

"Well, dear, I'm sure you'll feel better after a little rat nap. Wouldn't you like a mouthful of something first?"

"No, thank you," Montague said, pulling the covers back over his head.

Before long, he could hear his mother humming at her work again. As he dozed off, she was beginning to worry about running out of purple.

He dozed on and off for the next two days—and yet, strangely enough, the rest only exhausted him. All that time, his mother kept a vat of soup on the simmer. But whenever she heard him stir and brought over a tablespoon full, he pictured the wine trickling out of his uncle's snout and pushed the soup away. He'd never before gone more than a few hours without nibbling something, but now it had been days. In fact, he hadn't nibbled since before the trip to Pick-Person's gallery. He grew quite faint. On his third day in bed, his mother poked at him through the covers with the nib of a feather.

"My vats are all empty, Monty dear—no reds, no purples, no greens, no salmon-pinks, no yellows, nothing," she said pathetically. "Won't you be a sweet rat and eat something? If not for yourself, so you can have the strength to go get your poor mother some berries?"

He lifted a corner of the covers and peered out. His

mother looked so tragic that he decided to get up, once and for all. But when he tried to get out of bed, he was overcome by weakness and guilt and sorrow.

"Sorry, Mother." He sank back down with a sigh. "I don't have any energy."

The next morning his mother woke him early, before the ratlings' first screech. He could see that she hadn't slept a wink. There were inky circles under her eyes, making her gray face quite haggard-looking. "What's going to become of me without any dyes?" she groaned. "I don't know what to do with my paws. I guess I'll have to go myself—or ask your poor father. But it's been so long since either one of us has been in the park, I'm sure we'd end up lost."

"Oh, don't do that." Making a renewed effort to get out of bed, Montague found that he could no longer lift his head. How queer! He wasn't sleepy, yet he could hardly keep his eyes open. But when they closed, the whimpers of the ratlings seemed to turn to cheers, and he was back basking in the ovation of the rat world while his uncle, who deserved the cheers, was dying.

It was Tuesday, so that afternoon his mother went to meet Aunt Elizabeth's ship. When they returned, Montague opened one eye and peered out through a crack in his covers. Aunt Elizabeth was collapsed on her fancy French cigarette box. She was weeping, and her lovely face suddenly looked old.

Aunt Elizabeth's snifflings kept up all afternoon,

and Montague decided that the best way to atone for his uncle's death would be to let himself die, too. It would not, he suspected, take much longer. Every minute he felt fainter.

Suddenly someone was jiggling the bed. "This won't do, Monty," said his mother's voice. "You *must* eat."

He tried to shake his head but couldn't. "No, thank you," he whispered, just able to speak.

After a minute, he felt his covers pulled away. "Now, Monty, get up!" came Aunt Elizabeth's voice. "I brought you something."

He said nothing.

"Won't you show me what you did with the last shells I brought?"

"Over there," he whispered.

"Oh, yes. But you haven't gotten to them yet. Where are the others?"

"All gone."

"Gone? Where?"

In a voice so faint she had to put her ear to his snout, he gave her a brief version of his adventures while she'd been cruising around the Bahamas.

"So that's it," she said, stroking him between the ears. "And where does this Isabel Moberly-Rat live, where you left your shells?"

"Wharf 62," he whispered.

"My, that *is* grand," Aunt Elizabeth said sarcastically, one permanent address being as dreary as another to her. "Listen, Monty dear. You mustn't blame yourself for Moony. The way he drank, he wouldn't have lasted much longer anyway. The important thing is for you to carry on his name—and to be a good son to your poor mother. She's collapsed in a heap. She says if you waste away she'll throw all her hats in the East River."

He gave a faint grunt.

"That's a nice rat," she said. "Now, I brought you a couple of new shells. Once you're back on your paws, you'll paint them, won't you?"

But the thought of his shells, which had led to his uncle's death, was too much for him in his present condition. Tears rolled out of his closed eyes. They tickled his snout, but he was too drained even to scratch. He tried to blink—but couldn't. The whimpers of the ratlings faded into the distance. His breathing began to slow down. Soon it was slower than in his deepest winter sleeps. He made a final dreamlike attempt to twitch his tail—but nothing twitched.

He felt himself rising and knew he must be about to cross the gulf into the land of dead rats, where his uncle was. But interesting a sight as the gulf was sure to be, his eyes still wouldn't open. Then something warm was forced between his lips.

Montague swallowed a mouthful of porridge. Did a river of porridge run down the gulf between life and death? His mouth filled up again—gulp—and again! The warmth trickled down to his belly. His eyes man-

aged to struggle open. There, instead of the ghost of his uncle, was his father's face. His father was holding him in his paws as if he were a ratling—feeding him! How peculiar to be so close to his father, Montague thought dreamily. His father's paws felt very strong, rathletic, and he had sort of a nice smell, if a bit earthy. After force-feeding him half a vat of porridge, his father set him down, gave him a pat on the head, and then climbed back up the muddy, castle-ridden slope.

The warm food did its work quickly. Soon quite revived, Montague blinked around him. Two new rat's halos were leaning at the foot of the bed by the half-finished butterfly painting, but of Aunt Elizabeth and her cigarette box there wasn't a trace. His poor mother was collapsed by one of her empty dye vats, staring in his direction with a glazed expression.

"Don't worry, Mother," Montague said, remembering that he'd given Aunt Elizabeth his word, or at least his grunt, to be a good son. "I'll get you some berries tomorrow, and some feathers—I promise."

The next day was one of those hazy, humid mid-summer days when most creatures do their best not to stir. But Montague was true to his word. He dragged himself out of the gutter in Columbus Circle and crept up to the preening grounds above the reservoir in Central Park. When he had a full bouquet of feathers looped in his tail, he crept down to the berry patches by the Great Lawn. It occurred to him, as his cheeks began to bulge with berries, that he might look less ridiculous if in the future he copied Pembroke and found himself a pack for carrying the supplies. But then, what did he care if he looked undignified? All his old worries about being made fun of seemed child-ish and petty now, and he trudged straight out of the berry patch onto an open field, making no effort to keep out of sight.

But when he came out on the Sheep Meadow, he stopped short. It was sheepless, as usual, but there were an uncomfortable number of human beings there: the usual children with their mysterious balloons, along with a mob of grownups mysteriously lying out in the baking sun. Suddenly the air grew very still. It was almost as if the sky were holding its breath. Through the stillness came a faraway pattering, as of a rat scampering across a tin roof. Looking up, Montague watched a black cloud seep like spilled ink across the summer sky. Against the seeping blackness, the trees around the Sheep Meadow turned silvery, showing the undersides of their leaves. Thunder cracked. The sunbathers grabbed their towels and suntan oils and ran for cover. The children let go of their balloons and ran screaming after their parents. The balloons somersaulted into the sky. By the time the rain began to pelt down, bursting all the balloons and sweeping away all of Montague's feathers, he was the only creature left on the Sheep Meadow.

Or was he? The driving rain made him squint, so it was hard to see, but as he trotted after his feathers, he began to sense that he was not alone. He glanced sideways. A she-rat had fallen in at his side. Her fur was dripping and bedraggled, matted down unbecomingly.

"Isabel!"

"Gad!" said Isabel Moberly-Rat. "This is worse than the last one. And I *would* forget my new umbrella."

For the first time in several days, Montague cracked a smile. "And your ribbon," he remarked.

"Can you believe it, every one I have is shot! I've been . . . well, this will probably sound forward, but I've been out searching for you. And look at you, now that I've found you! You and your berries!" As she laughed, he spat out the berries and wiped his snout. "Do you know a place where we can get out of the rain?" she went on. "Somewhere other than a gutter?" She lifted a paw to her ribbonless neck. "Frankly, I've had it up to here with gutters."

"I know a bush, Isabel. Up by the reservoir."

Leafy as it was, Montague's laurel bush provided only indifferent shelter from the rain. But as they crouched side by side beneath it, watching the drops pock and wrinkle the skin of the water, neither of them much minded getting wet. And as it turned out, the storm was only one of those brief tantrums Nature throws to break the summertime boredom—over almost before it begins. The pelting rain turned to the gentle ping of drops spilling from leaves. The sun came out fresher than before, sparkling on the water. Birds swooped among the trees, singing with all their hearts, as if celebrating the creation of a brand-new world.

"I know birds aren't too bright," Isabel remarked after a while. "But they really are lovely, don't you think?"

But far lovelier than any bird, in Montague's opinion, was the bedraggled rat beside him. Shyly, he told her so.

"You really think so?" Isabel said. "Will you do my portrait, then?"

"Oh . . . but I've given up painting."

"What! But don't be silly, Montague!" And then, more gently: "I mean, won't you—for me?"

"Well . . . maybe . . . for you."

Something twined around his tail. Glancing back, he saw to his utter astonishment that it was *her* tail.

"Why, what's that?" he asked, noticing a flash of silver.

"That? That's from your Aunt Elizabeth."

"Aunt Elizabeth?" he said, amazed. But indeed, it was Aunt Elizabeth's ring, worked with suns and phases of the moon. "How in the world do you know Aunt Elizabeth?"

"Oh, she dropped by our crate yesterday. I was a complete wreck—I'd been out beating the bushes for you again—but she was very sweet and understanding. She wouldn't tell me where you live. She said there wasn't much of a horizon down there and she thought we ought to meet where there *was* one. But she made me a present of this ring and told me she hoped I'd do it more justice than she had. It's absolutely the loveliest thing I've ever seen, Montague—except your paintings."

All this time, her tail remained boldly twined in his. The glowing, twilit water seemed to overrun its

banks and spill into Montague's heart. But after a
while the sunset colors in the sky melted and ran
down behind the horizon. The birds finished the last
movement of their symphony. Night settled over the
park, and Montague's sadness crept back into him.
Somewhere beneath them, Uncle Moony was buried,
but the rainstorm had wiped out whatever mark the
rats had left on his grave.

"I wish . . ." he began. Then he sighed.

"I know," Isabel said. "But just think, he's part of rat history now."

He looked at her gratefully. "But only as a name."

"That's true, I guess. They won't really know him." She sighed, too. "I wish I could remember the words to one of his songs."

'I heard him sing one once." Montague tightened his tail in hers as he stared out at the moon. For one instant the blurry, darkish splotch on the face of the moon came clear, clear enough that he would be able to paint it from memory, if he ever wanted to. It was the silhouette of a mangy rat.

Montague sang softly:

> Rings are round the sun and moon,
>   And inside of trees;
> Some are made by angel rats,
>   Some in factories.

He stopped singing, thinking of the coincidence of how he'd been inside a tree himself when the multitude of rats had caught up with him. "That's all I remember."

"Mmmm, it's sort of like a lullaby," Isabel said dreamily. "Are you sleepy?"

He admitted that he was. "I guess it's time to go, isn't it? Poor Mother. She's expecting me with feathers and berries."

To his surprise, Isabel didn't release his tail. "We

could get them in the morning," she suggested after a moment. "If I helped, we could get double. Can't you see me with my cheeks full of berries!"

"You mean, stay here all night?"

"Well, it's not a bad spot."

"But, Isabel, you might catch cold. You got drenched."

"Oh, but I'm fine now. I've never felt warmer in my life."

"Me neither," he murmured, not at all sorry to lose the argument.

When she kissed him good night, it was as if he'd already floated out across the water into a dream; and soon he did float off into a pleasant dream, for the active day had tired him after his fasting. It took Isabel a bit longer to fall asleep. She'd heard that vicious rats roamed this part of the park at night, and just as she was dozing off, something rustled in the bushes behind them. She crept even closer to Montague's side and pricked up her ears. But there were no other scary noises, and after a while her lids drooped shut on the moonlight, and she, too, drifted into a blissful sleep.

She might not have drifted off so peacefully if she'd turned around at the rustling sound and seen the pair of rat's eyes peering out from under the next bush— for the eyes were rather shifty and yellowish. But she did drift off, and once she fell sound asleep, her tail relaxed, untwining from the other. Stealthy as a cat, the spying rat sidled out from under the neighboring bush and slid something silver onto Montague's tail. It matched the one on the young she-rat's tail perfectly.

The spy crept back to the other bush, hoisted a paper bag onto his back, and slouched off along the bank of the reservoir. The bag jingled with new treasures of various sorts, paper clips and nickels and bottle caps, but nothing nearly so valuable and shiny as what he'd just given away. Painful as it had been, however, he now understood what had made him lurk back there to do that piece of business. It wasn't such a crummy deal. For he now felt the most surprising sensation, tingling sweetly from his snout to his tail, as if he'd just been dipped clean in those moonlit waters.

In fact, the feeling made Pembroke want to sing, of all things! He'd never been one for that sort of nonsense—besides which, his voice was scratchy even for a pack rat's. But the truth of it was he'd been missing his old partner a bit more than he'd expected these last few days, and once he was far enough away not to disturb the sleepers, he managed to croak out the second verse of his old friend's song:

> *Some rings hoop around the heart,*
> *From a lover, or a friend;*
> *But all are circles—none begin,*
> *And none will ever end.*